TAKING THE
TITANIC

JAMES PATTERSON is one of the best-known and biggest-selling writers of all time. His books have sold in excess of 325 million copies worldwide and he has been the most borrowed author in UK libraries for the past nine years in a row. He is the author of some of the most popular series of the past two decades – the Alex Cross, Women's Murder Club, Detective Michael Bennett and Private novels – and he has written many other number one bestsellers including romance novels and stand-alone thrillers.

James is passionate about encouraging children to read. Inspired by his own son who was a reluctant reader, he also writes a range of books for young readers including the Middle School, I Funny, Treasure Hunters, House of Robots, Confessions and Maximum Ride series. James is the proud sponsor of the World Book Day Award and has donated millions in grants to independent bookshops. He lives in Florida with his wife and son.

D0774672

BOOK**SHOTS**

STORIES AT THE SPEED OF LIFE

What you are holding in your hands right now is no ordinary book, it's a BookShot.

BookShots are page-turning stories by James Patterson and other writers that can be read in one sitting.

Each and every one is fast-paced, 100% story-driven; a shot of pure entertainment guaranteed to satisfy.

Available as new, compact paperbacks, ebooks and audio, everywhere books are sold.

BookShots - the ultimate form of storytelling. From the ultimate storyteller.

TAKING THE
TITANIC

JAMES
PATTERSON

WITH *SCOTT SLAVEN*

BOOK**SHOTS**

1 3 5 7 9 10 8 6 4 2

BookShots
20 Vauxhall Bridge Road
London SW1V 2SA

BookShots is part of the Penguin Random House
group of companies whose addresses can be found at
global.penguinrandomhouse.com

Penguin
Random House
UK

Copyright © James Patterson 2016

The BookShots name and logo are a trademark of JBP Business, LLC.

James Patterson has asserted his right to be identified as the author of this
Work in accordance with the Copyright, Designs and Patents Act 1988.

This is a work of fiction. All characters and descriptions of events are the
products of the author's imagination and any resemblance to
actual persons is entirely coincidental

First published by BookShots in 2016

www.penguin.co.uk

A CIP catalogue record for this book is available from the British Library.

ISBN 9781786531087

Printed and bound in Great Britain by Clays Ltd, St Ives Plc

MIX
Paper from
responsible sources
FSC® C018179

Penguin Random House is committed to a sustainable future for our
business, our readers and our planet. This book is made from Forest
Stewardship Council® certified paper.

TAKING THE
TITANIC

CHAPTER 1

Nigel Bowen
Southampton
Tuesday, April 9, 1912, 11:00 PM

THE ONLY THING that could save me was a losing hand.

Holding my breath, I slowly lifted my cards: *full house*.

I was a dead man.

I glanced around the table at my fellow players, then around the dark bar. There were only ten or so other patrons in the squalid place, and it smelled of beer, sweat, and urine—unfortunately, in reverse order.

All eyes were on me. I'd never had this kind of winning streak before—I couldn't lose to save my life, quite literally. These toughs had obviously thought a swell coming into a dingy saloon like this one was an easy mark. But instead, I'd taken everything they had. And I doubted they would let me get away with it.

As I hesitated, the player next to me—Lennie, a mean, short little man—saw me look over at the pretty red-haired whore seated at the bar.

"Keep your mind on the cards, mate!" Lennie hissed. The other players grunted in agreement, but I noticed their eyes wandering, too. She was worth looking at: slim, full bosom, big blue eyes, and a sort of permanent half smile that said she knew *exactly* what a fellow was thinking.

There was nothing I could do but put down my cards.

You'd have thought I fired a revolver. At the sight of my hand, fists pounded the table and the men's faces reddened with fury.

"Who's this bloke think he is comin' in here takin' *our* money?" Lennie barked to the others.

But before any of the players could grab their weapon of choice, the woman loudly shoved her stool from the bar. It clattered to the floor with a bang, stopping all conversation.

"Hold up, gents," she commanded. She slowly strode toward the table, hands on her hips with a haughty air. Lennie and the others were turned into schoolboys, struck dumb by her beauty and contempt. Without taking her eyes off the table, she reached down into the startled Lennie's lap and lifted something—a playing card.

"What's this then?" she asked, revealing a heavy Cockney accent. Lennie's eyes bugged out and he visibly paled, shooting a look at his mates.

"It ain't mine! I swear on me mother's—"

Oskar, a weathered Swede who had bet and lost the most in the course of the game, slammed a fist into Lennie's mouth. The other players leapt forward across the table, overturning it and knocking the woman to the floor. The small bar crowd erupted into delighted cheers—not in support of any one player but for the sport of a brawl. Beer mugs slammed against heads, bodies tumbled, and obscenities were howled.

I dodged a flying whiskey bottle only to see Oskar lunging toward me. But the prostitute threw her leg up, tripping him to fall face-first into a splintered wooden support beam. Knocked out, he fell with his face sliding down the column; by the time he reached the floor, his face was shredded.

I reached down and pulled the woman to her feet. Together, we ran for the exit and made it out just before a wine cask smashed into the door, shattering the front glass panel and sending wood splintering in every direction.

We paused in the middle of the rainy, gaslit street. I was new to Southampton and guessed that unless we were prepared to jump into the bay, our best escape was to head away from the docks. Indeed, my companion pulled me in that direction, and, at her mercy, I followed.

She led me down a maze of treeless, grimy streets at a run until at last we came to a two-story warehouse. As we folded into the darkened doorway, I looked around apprehensively. Though the streets seemed deserted, I had a strange certainty that we had been followed. A sudden scream—a woman's—pierced the night.

"Nice hiding place you've chosen," I muttered.

"Nice playmates you chose, luv," she said, and gave me an appraising glance up and down.

"True, I overestimated their commitment to good sportsmanship," I said. "Thankfully, Lady Luck was on my side."

She snorted a laugh. "That I was, dearie."

She reached into her cloak and pulled something out. "And it's bloody lucky I have sharp eyesight. You flashed the card I was meant to find so fast I couldn't tell if it was an ace of hearts or diamonds."

She flipped the card she was holding over—a diamond. I grinned.

"Actually, it was supposed to be a heart, but it obviously didn't matter. The gentlemen saw red and that was enough," I observed. "Well, it was a good plan, but I'm afraid all we ended up with is our necks intact and our pockets empty."

She gave me another lingering look and seemed to be making her mind up about something. Finally, she reached into her cloak again and pulled out—to my astonishment—a fistful of cash.

"You got my winnings?" I gasped, as I reached for the bills.

She pulled the pistol out of her cloak so quickly it seemed to have materialized by sorcery.

"*Our* winnings, luv," she warned, nudging the end of the gun into my chest. I held my hands up sheepishly and she put it away to begin counting out the bills.

"How fortunate that we met today," I said, accepting my share. "But I'm still curious as to why you approached me."

"And I'm still curious what a bloke of your class is doin' down here."

I shrugged, trying to look innocent. "Hoping to meet a charming lass such as yourself."

"Ha. I don't usually work wiv partners, but you aren't half bad," she said. "In fact, I've got somethin' a bit grander on me mind. Care to hear…?"

She turned away to look down the waterfront. Far down the seemingly never-ending docks, a massive dark shape was barely outlined in the dim night sky—but it shone with rows of glittering lights. It took a moment for me to recognize the stacked decks of an impossibly magnificent ocean liner, the one all of Southampton was buzzing about: the RMS *Titanic*.

CHAPTER 2

Celia Bowen
Southampton
Wednesday, April 10, 1912, 10:30 AM

"IS THIS YOUR first time sailing, miss?"

"*'Mrs.'* Yes, my husband and I are on our honeymoon," I replied to the little vicar at my side, as I scanned the huge crowd milling about the boarding area. "At least I think we are—he went to check on our tickets *ages* ago. Perhaps I've been jilted!"

I laughed lightly, but I began to wonder if, after eagerly agreeing to the plan the previous night, my new partner had decided against it after all. He had seemed awfully jumpy this morning when he picked me up, but then again, I knew very little about him. Somehow the thought gave me an involuntary shiver—though it might also have been due to the brisk afternoon. I pulled my cream silk jacket closer. With the line in front of me, I was doomed to at least another fifteen minutes of the vicar's chattering.

"You couldn't have picked a finer ship!" he droned. "Not only the largest and most luxurious, but also the *safest.*"

I glanced up. The four blood-red smoke funnels towered up above us as high as Big Ben. From the stern to bow the ship seemed to go on forever—endless windows that finally came to the bow where simple block letters in gold were emblazoned: TITANIC.

"Yes, the *Titanic* is a beauty—not unlike you, my dear!" the vicar smiled as he moved in closer. "It might be unseemly for a man of the cloth to say this, but I've never seen such extraordinary blond hair. As if made of cotton candy!"

I smiled politely; I'd been hearing the same line since I was thirteen.

"Sorry, darling, you wouldn't believe the crowds."

I turned to the tall man with the bushy black hair and a dashing moustache; in fact, all the nearby women turned toward him. Nigel cut quite a figure in his pin-striped suit and brightly colored bow tie.

"I was afraid you'd changed your mind," I said tartly, though inside I was almost faint with relief. I turned to the vicar. "This is my husband, Nigel Bowen."

"Delighted, sir!" the vicar exclaimed. Nigel nodded and flashed the grin that I had already seen charm shopgirls and cabbies alike. He then turned to me.

"I'm sorry, Celia, but first class is completely booked. We'll have to stay in second class, after all."

"Oh Nigel! You *promised!*" I said with a little stamp of my foot.

Nigel shrugged apologetically and took my gloved hand and kissed it.

The line surged closer to the front, and suddenly we heard a newspaper boy shouting from the edges of the crowd: *"Southampton Streetwalker Strangled! Vicious Killer on the Loose! Read all about it now!"*

I couldn't help myself and gasped out loud.

"Oh, how awful!" the vicar said with concern. "He really shouldn't be shouting such shocking matters in front of ladies."

I looked over at Nigel, who was fumbling with our tickets and suddenly dropped them. When he picked it up I saw that his hands were shaking.

"Why can't they move this line along?" he sighed with annoyance.

Just then a large man with epaulets on his shoulders and official-looking badges on his jacket approached us.

"Mr. Bowen? Mr. Nigel Bowen?" he inquired.

Nigel glanced at me in a funny kind of way before answering.

"Yes? Yes, what do you want?"

"I've good news, sir. A young woman in First Class has…well, ahem," he stumbled as glanced nervously at me. "Her, um, *time* has come earlier than expected so her husband has taken her to the mothers' ward. Their cabin is available should you still like to change to First Class accommodations."

"Oh, how splendid for you!" the vicar all but shouted. "Though I am sorry to lose such delightful companions!"

We nodded to the little man, and Nigel led me along after the ticketing official.

"Is this ship still leaving on time?" Nigel asked him, impatiently. "I don't see how you'll get all these people on board in the next hour."

I glanced over at him. "I wouldn't have guessed you were such a nervous traveler, *dear*."

"Oh, we'll be on time," the official said. "The White Star line prides itself on punctuality."

The first class boarding area wasn't as crowded as second but there seemed to be just as much excitement in the air. As I was telling a porter that our baggage needed to be moved to our new room, I overheard the official say to Nigel, "We'll have to hurry but we just have time to change the names on the passenger list. Your wife's na—"

"Oh, don't bother with all that," Nigel said, with irritation. Then he quickly changed his tone to a "we're old pals" manner. "We don't mind travelling under an alias— it's rather romantic!"

The official looked curiously at Nigel. "I'm sorry sir, that's not protocol. The White Star line prides itself on our accuracy—"

"And what a wonderful job you do!" Nigel exclaimed as he pulled his billfold out. "We so much appreciate how you've accommodated us with our new digs. Above and beyond the call of duty and all that!"

Nigel patted him on the back with one hand and, with the other, took the man's hand to shake it—and to slip him a hundred-dollar bill. The official looked down at his hand and paused. Then he smiled up at Nigel and said, "Well…I do hope you enjoy your crossing, Mr.—er, Bjornstrom. Happy sailing!"

He lifted his cap to me and trotted off.

Nigel took my arm. "Let's hurry, my love. We don't want to have to tell our grandchildren we missed the *Titanic*'s maiden voyage…"

CHAPTER 3

Nigel Bowen
English Channel
Wednesday, April 10, 1912, 7:30 PM

ALL EYES WERE on Celia when we entered into the First Class Dining Saloon on D Deck. As it was the first night out, everyone was still in traveling clothes, yet Celia still managed to look like she'd stepped out of a fashion magazine. Her maroon plumed hat put the finishing touch on a simple outfit consisting of a short vest over a blouse with a full wool skirt. I felt a tinge of pride that she was on my arm and causing such a stir.

We paused to take in the lavish features of the white-paneled dining room: intricately molded plaster on the ceilings, a tile design on the floor that was arranged to resemble a Persian rug, leather club chairs, and small lanterns on every table. Our cabin steward had told us that the dining saloon held five hundred people, yet it looked like easily twice that number was here this night.

A stiff maître d' approached us with a clipboard containing the seating list.

"Mr. and Mrs.—er, *Bjornstrom?*" he asked, tripping over the pronunciation.

"Eh, close enough," I said as he led us to a table—the largest one in the room. I very much wanted a drink, as I had all afternoon, since being flooded with relief when we *finally* pulled out of the dock. At the table, one of the top ranking officers was seated at the head, indicating this was an elite group. Attention from the ship's crew was not something I would have opted for, but changing tables would have only made matters worse. We were seated and various introductions made. An obviously wealthy woman in her late fifties—a Mrs. Beryl Sedgwick—with small spectacles perched on her long nose, openly stared at Celia.

After a moment the woman said in a haughty manner, "I feel certain we've met before. But it must have been before your marriage as I am not familiar with the name Bjornstrom."

Celia smiled with ease. "I don't believe I've had the pleasure of your acquaintance, Mrs. Sedgwick, whether under my family name, my husband's name…or Mr. Bjornstrom's."

The old bird was clearly taken aback and murmurs went around the table. Celia turned to me with a wide-eyed innocent look—one that seemed to contain a dare.

"My wife is having a little fun," I spoke up with a laugh. "Mr. and Mrs. Bjornstrom had to cancel their travel at the last moment, and we secured their cabin. It seemed silly to make a fuss about changing the passenger list. I'm Nigel Bowen and this lovely creature is my wife, Celia."

"Oh, now I'm sorry I gave the game away," Celia mused. "We could have sailed incognito for the entire voyage. I would have played Mrs. Bjornstrom as very severe and chilly. I might even have claimed Swedish royalty!"

The other diners laughed good-naturedly—except for Mrs. Sedgwick. She continued studying Celia.

"Can we surmise then that you've had experience on the stage, Mrs....?" Sedgwick asked, deliberately leaving off the last name.

"*Bowen*. And no, I've never acted onstage," Celia said. "Have *you?*"

"Certainly *not!*" Mrs. Sedgwick gasped, shocked to the core. The other diners had to stifle laughter.

The rest of the meal went smoothly—all *ten* courses. Conversation centered mostly on the magnificence of the ship, which the officer was glad to supplement with miscellaneous facts: "RMS" stood for "Royal Mail Steamer," and the ship was carrying over three thousand mailbags— in fact, mail was second only to the passengers in terms of precious cargo; there was an onboard telephone system; and, most important, there were twenty thousand bottles of beer and stout onboard. Amid the talk, a young man at the far end of the table started to mention the lurid murder in Southampton but was silenced with one steely glare from Mrs. Sedgwick.

Celia charmed everyone—particularly a Mr. Randolph Davies. Though he had to be in his mid-seventies, the paunchy and white-bearded Davies looked Celia up and down as lustily as a college boy. He was one of the most prominent members of New York City's moneyed class, probably just a few million shy of the likes of John Jacob Astor IV, who sat with his wife at a more private table with the *Titanic*'s captain, Edward Smith.

"Would any of you gentlemen care for a game of cards?" I asked with a direct look at Davies.

"Oh, Nigel!" Celia sighed. "On our very *first* night out?"

Several of the men—including Davies—instantly agreed. As we were getting up from the table, one of the younger women, Mrs. Minahan, spoke up.

"Honestly, the very least you gentlemen could do is pay attention to we ladies for *one* night of this voyage!" she said in a flat American accent. "How shall we exact our revenge on them, Mrs. Bowen?"

She looked expectantly at Celia, who was busily digging in her handbag and didn't look up. An awkward moment passed.

"Darling, Mrs. Minahan is speaking to you," I said gently.

"*What?*" Celia asked, startled. "Oh, I'm so sorry. When

I can't find my face powder I'm all at sea—quite literally in this case!"

Celia laughed in her best sparkling manner, but I looked at the other end of the table and saw Mrs. Sedgwick staring just as intently as ever at her.

"All blushing young brides have to become accustomed to their new name at some point, my dear," she said with sugar-coated venom. "Perhaps once you settle upon one it will grow easier...."

CHAPTER 4

Nigel Bowen

English Channel

Wednesday, April 10, 1912, 9:30 PM

I SAT BACK in a huge velvet-covered club chair and told my fellow players that my luck at cards must have been left ashore: I'd lost every hand we'd played. Davies was delighted with my losing streak, and I could tell the others saw me as a rank amateur.

I was even outdone by a friendly young sportsman with a thatch of white-blond hair, Philip Colley, who kept urging me to "Buck up!" and even said, "That's the way, old chap!" when I managed a hand with two meager sevens. He again brought up the previous night's murder.

"Ghastly business that strangulation, eh?" he asked excitedly.

"Just a streetwalker," one of the other men noted dryly. "There's plenty to take her place."

"Come now, old man," Phil protested. "That's rather cold. The poor creature deserves some pity."

As there was none to be found at the table, I quickly started to deal another hand.

"The girl was found in a hotel room belonging to a *gentleman*," Phil went on. "And it seems the proprietor gave the police a pretty clear description of the killer. A youngish chap, tall and bearded and—"

Two cards flew out of my hand, causing all to look at me with surprise.

"Looks like I'm still finding my sea legs." I shrugged and hurriedly dealt on.

We played for another few minutes until Mrs. Davies, a statuesque woman who looked after her husband like a hawk, came over and demanded that he escort her to their cabin. I was paying my losses just as Celia approached with Mrs. Minahan and Mrs. Sedgwick.

"Nigel! Don't tell me you were *betting* again?" Celia cried.

As I hung my head in mock guilt, she playfully slapped my arm. Turning to the other ladies, she said, "He's convinced he's the world's greatest gambler—despite *very* strong evidence to the contrary. It's a wonder he's ever able to buy me a nice trinket now and then—like this darling little diamond bracelet he just picked up in Dublin!"

Celia lifted her wrist to show off the piece—but her arm was bare. She confusedly looked at her other arm, which was also naked.

"Oh, my!" she cried. "But I could have *sworn* I put it on this evening!"

"You were absolutely wearing a bracelet earlier, my dear," Mrs. Davies assured her. "I noticed it—as I'm sure my husband did while gazing at you!"

Old Davies, flustered at the jibe, tried to take charge. "Well, the blasted thing must have fallen off. I'll have a look under the table."

Straining his aged knees, Davies bent down to look under the table, as did several of the others. Celia tittered away in worry.

"I *knew* I should have had the clasp reinforced," she said.

I motioned a steward over and soon the search party had swelled to at least ten. But no bracelet was found— only a shilling and small box of tablets for the relief of those suffering from "excessive wind."

"Don't fret, darling," I said to Celia. "It's only a piece of jewelry. I'll find another for you."

"But *where* is it?" she cried. "Someone surely must have found it. I can't imagine anyone being so cruel as to keep it!"

The other ladies comforted Celia. Even Mrs. Sedgwick patted her arm.

"It may still turn up," I assured her. "Unless one of our fellow diners helped themselves to it between courses five and six!"

I laughed a bit too loudly and several of the women looked at me askance.

"Really, Mr. Bowen!" said Mrs. Sedgwick, indignant. "I think making light of your wife's distress is in very poor taste indeed, not to mention your implication that someone of our class would resort to thievery."

With a toss of her head, Mrs. Sedgwick indicated that my gaffe had ended the evening. Taking Celia gently by the shoulders, she steered her out of the room with the others following. Phil gave me a good-natured pat on the back.

"Going in, Mr. Bowen?" he asked.

I shook my head. "No, I think I'll take a stroll and enjoy a cigar. And give my wife time to regain herself."

"Mrs. Bowen is pretty as a Ziegfeld girl! I hope you don't think that rude."

I nodded my acceptance of his compliment and together we walked onto the deck. First class occupied the center of the ship, where there was the least roll; in fact, the ship barely seemed to be moving. But as we leaned against the railing and looked down, we saw that the liner was effortlessly plowing through the dark English Channel. Phil took out a lighter and held it up toward me. I pulled out my cigar case and, opening it, nodded up at the four smoke funnels that towered over us.

"I'm told the original design of this ship was for only three funnels," I noted. "The fourth was added to give the ship greater majesty. But it's just an air vent."

As Philip looked up curiously, I quickly moved the diamond bracelet from my cigar case to my coat pocket.

"I say!" Philip marveled. "Who would expect such deception on the *Titanic*?"

Suppressing a smile, I leaned forward for a light.

"No one."

CHAPTER 5

Celia Bowen
Celtic Sea
Thursday, April 11, 1912, 8:00 AM

"*MORE* PEOPLE ARE getting on the ship? But won't it sink?"

Everyone nearby laughed, angering the little boy who frowned at all of us.

We were enjoying the morning in the elegant and very private First Class Promenade, an enclosed deck area with Tudor-style wood paneling. An assortment of chairs faced out to sea, and though there was a nip in the air outside, the promenade was sun-drenched and cheerful. I thought it amusing how our dinner companions from last night had already formed something of a clique and hung together.

"It's not funny!" the child insisted, stamping his foot. "My dog, Ladybelle, is below deck and I don't think she can swim."

I knelt down to the stern-faced boy. "All dogs can swim," I insisted. "But there's no need to worry; the *Titanic* is the world's first *unsinkable* ship!"

Unconvinced, the boy turned toward his father—a tall, bookish man named Herbert Vogel—who smiled at his child. "It's true, Arthur. The *Titanic* could take on ten times as many people as she'll pick up in Queenstown this morning and still stay afloat!"

I wandered over to the window and then glanced down the deck where Nigel was chatting with a rather demure girl, Miss Emily Moore. From the pleased way she looked up at Nigel from her deck chair it was clear he was flirting. Her surprisingly elderly father, Langston Moore, was standing with them and openly glaring at Nigel. I wondered why Nigel was putting so much effort into charming the two when Mr. Moore had stated—over and over again—that he did *not* approve of card playing.

"My dear, I was so touched by your distress at the loss of your bracelet."

I turned to see Mr. Davies standing at my side—or, more accurately, *pressing* against my side. I took a step back and did my best to smile in response to his leer. With his carefully swept back white hair and dapper morning suit, he looked as respectable as a judge—but I knew his type. And apparently his wife did, too, as I noted she kept one eye on him from across the deck.

"That's kind of you, Mr. Davies," I said. "But I'm afraid I made far too much of the loss. As my husband said, it's just a piece of jewelry and can be replaced."

He leaned forward again, so close I could smell the coffee on his breath.

"Oh, I assure you, my dear, it can be *very* easily replaced," he said, taking my hand in his. With a glance over at his wife, who was now animatedly telling a story, he used his other hand to quickly but forcefully squeeze my breast.

I slapped him so hard his head smacked against the window we were standing in front of.

I don't know which of us was the more shocked. His face instantly went beet-red, and for a moment I had the idea he was going to fall to the ground. Shaking with anger, I staggered past him to the far side of the promenade. I didn't know if any of the others had seen, and for the moment I didn't care.

"I say, are you all right?"

It was the young fair-haired fellow, Philip Colley—wide-eyed with concern.

"That old coot deserves to be tossed overboard!" he exclaimed with his fists clenched at his side.

"Oh, Mr. Colley, forget what you saw," I begged him. "I don't know what came over me."

"You did what any self-respecting woman would have in your position—but not one in twenty would have the nerve!" he said, looking at me with astonished admiration.

"Mr. Davies forgot himself; it happens with men of his class," I said simply.

"Oh, he knew exactly what he was doing. Just because of

his social standing he thinks he can take liberties!" the boy fumed.

I smiled at his naiveté. "It's the way of the world, Mr. Colley. Say nothing about it. My husband would not be pleased to learn that I've angered his chief card companion. Let it be our secret."

Despite his outrage he seemed delighted to be in my confidence. I held out my hand and, eyes shining, he took it.

Together, we walked back down the deck toward the others. Mr. Davies had obviously collected himself. He now held a map and was making a great show of explaining the route we were sailing to his wife, Mrs. Sedgwick, and little Arthur Vogel. He did not look our way as we walked by.

Just ahead, I saw Miss Moore start to rise from her deck chair. Nigel and Mr. Moore simultaneously bent down to help her up—and knocked against each other. Mr. Moore reared backward, and for the second time that morning I expected to see an elderly man fall to the deck.

But Nigel reached out and firmly gripped the older man's arm, righting his stance but jostling his coat in the process. Mr. Moore's billfold flipped out of his open jacket and landed on the deck. Flustered, he huffed and started to bend over, but Nigel was too quick for him. He picked up the billfold and, first waving it in the air as though performing a magician's trick, he presented it to the furious older man with both hands.

Mr. Moore—frowning with greater hostility than ever—begrudgingly took the billfold. I watched as Nigel then smilingly held out one hand to Miss Moore and, with his other, thrust a wad of bills into his trouser pocket.

CHAPTER 6

Celia Bowen
Celtic Sea
Thursday, April 11, 1912, 1:00 PM

"FUNNY THAT YOU'RE missing a bracelet. I seem to have misplaced a very nice gold watch."

I was having a post-luncheon walk around the deck with my new protector, Mr. Colley, or Phil, as he begged me to call him. The ship was rocking slightly and we kept bumping into each other as we awkwardly moved along. After we had eaten, Nigel had insisted on another game of cards with the men. The other ladies had pleaded with me to join them in an afternoon of sewing and empty chatter, but Phil had rescued me with the offer of a stroll. I accepted so quickly the ladies' eyebrows went up practically in unison.

"Oh, dear," I cried. "Have you reported it to the crew?"

A strained look came across Phil's face for a moment.

"Well…no. I haven't. I don't think I will. Anyway, perhaps it will turn up at some point—along with your bit of jewelry, I hope."

I looked at him curiously. "But why wouldn't you report

it? Someone is bound to find it and turn it in. It's a hope I cling to!"

Phil chewed his bottom lip and looked out at the gleaming ocean water.

"Well, you see…it's from a lady friend," he said with an attempt at extreme tact. "And—well, this is awkward—but, you see, her family isn't aware of our…friendship. And there's a rather personal message inscribed on the back of the watch. It's all such a bother."

"Oh, how romantic!" I smiled.

Phil turned to me with the earnestness that only a twenty-two-year-old college boy can express. "Yes, I thought it was. But now…"

He looked at me with such lovesick eyes it took every ounce of restraint I had not to giggle. I pressed his arm.

"You're very, very sweet," I said.

He thrust his hands in his pockets, and we walked past the crowded gymnasium.

"I suppose I have my nerve. Cursing out old Davies for making a pass at you, then I go ahead and make just as big a fool of myself," he said miserably.

I stopped him and said with as much sincerity as I could, "You've paid me a very dear compliment and at a time when I needed one. Thank you."

We stopped in front of the smoking room. The warm light of the interior made the outside deck seem rather cold. A roar of hilarity came from inside, and we saw Nigel seated across the room at the card table. His hands were thrown up in the air in resignation while the other men laughingly shook their heads at what was clearly his continuing bad luck.

"Mr. Bowen, he…" Phil stammered. "Well, he certainly takes his losses with good humor."

"He's certainly had a lot of practice lately!" I said with a tight edge in my voice. "If he keeps at it, we'll be in steerage by the end of this voyage."

Phil's brow furrowed. "Look, if you need…well, *anything*."

"What I *need*," I insisted with a carefree wave, "is to do a better job of distracting my husband from the card table. And to make sure no more of my few good possessions go missing."

We had come to a hallway entrance and Phil opened the door with a thoughtful look.

"It is odd that we both have lost a valuable early in the passage," he noted as we approached the door to my cabin. "I suppose theft is possible. Of course, it would have to be a crew member. A few of them do look rather shady. But at least you and I can trust each other—that's something!"

He again looked deep into my eyes and I was afraid for a moment that he was going to try to kiss me. But he caught himself and pulled back with obvious embarrassment.

"And your husband, too, of course," he said with a strained smile. "That goes without saying."

"Yes," I said. "That goes without saying…."

CHAPTER 7

Nigel Bowen
Atlantic Ocean
Thursday, April 11, 1912, 2:30 PM

"I LOST ANOTHER thousand dollars," I announced as I entered the cabin. "At least I think so. I still find the conversion from pounds to dollars most vexing."

Celia's back was to me as she was sitting at her vanity table. I began removing my day clothes, folding each piece neatly over the chair near the bed. Ours was one of the modest first class cabins. Besides the bed and vanity, there was a writing desk, a bureau, and a rather small sofa. But all was done in flawlessly carved and stained mahogany. Amid the opulence, my eye caught something glittering under the lamplight on the desk. I wandered over and, picking it up, I judged the weight—which was hefty—and turned it over.

"'Yes, You may call me Sweetheart. Yours, Lilith.'" I read the inscription on the back of the gold watch aloud with amusement. I then began singing the popular song loudly. *"Let me call you sweetheart, I'm in love with you! Let me hear you whisper that you love me, too!"*

"You seem to be as bad at singing as you are at gambling," Celia said with a shudder.

"Alas, that is my true singing voice," I confessed. "But after last night and today, I've lost enough that I've firmly established my card-playing incompetence. And so tonight, the inexplicable winning streak starts."

I walked behind her and watched for a moment as she adjusted a bit of face powder. She glanced up at me questioningly in the mirror.

"I think I prefer you as a redhead," I said. "I also miss the Cockney accent."

"Coo', but it took me ever so long to talk good 'n' proper, guv," she said, laying it on thick. "Also, that red wig itched dreadfully."

I again tested the heft of the watch. "Miss Lilith must be devoted to young Phil. She spent a pretty sum on this. Is he heartbroken over the loss?"

Celia shrugged. "He's just a boy. I doubt his affections run very deep."

Turning around, she said, "By the way, don't think I haven't noticed that you've yet to return my bracelet, husband dear—*nor* have you given me half the spoils you lifted from Mr. Moore."

I went over to the bureau and fished the delicate piece out of a drawer. I tossed it across the room and Celia caught it without the slightest effort.

"You've a remarkably steady hand, darling," I said. "I've been impressed by it ever since you pulled a gun on me."

"I've still got that gun," she remarked. "So watch yourself."

Sitting in the chair, I pulled off my shoes. "I have to admit I've had my doubts about this scheme," I told her. "Posing as swells to rob the other swells aboard the world's greatest ship. And yet it's working wonderfully! Just mind you keep that bracelet out of sight—it's our best defense against suspicion."

She reached under the bed and pulled out one of her great hatboxes. She parted the silken interior lining and slipped the bracelet inside. Without looking at me she asked, "Why are you staring at me?"

I laughed at her uncanny perception. "I'm still trying to figure you out. I've so many questions. Why the elaborate disguise and accent that night? Why did you choose me as your accomplice? Why hasn't such an extraordinarily beautiful woman been snapped up by some rich bloke by now?"

"I haven't asked many questions of you," Celia volleyed back. "Such as why adopt the Bjornstroms' name? And what were you really doing in that part of town the other night? An area, I might add, where a woman was murdered...."

I sat up straight as a board. "Do you...suspect me?"

She paused for a beat and then shrugged. "I don't see how you would have had the time."

"Hmm, I'd rather you thought it wasn't in my character, but I'll take what I can get," I said. "It amuses me to speculate on *your* character. I have two theories on your mysterious identity. One: you're an exotic spy, pursued by Scotland Yard because you've made off with top-secret documents from Parliament. Two: you're a member of the Royal Family and, frustrated with your life of privilege and the tedious duties of your rank, you've opted for the glamour of a life of crime!"

"You've read too many dime novels," she said, smiling despite herself.

"Darling! I may be a thief," I admitted. "But I make it point to steal only from the best. Those plots come from the classics of literature! Or the nickelodeon—I can never quite remember which."

Celia pulled down the bed quilt and cast off her light robe.

"I need to rest up a bit before I face another dinner with those awful busybodies," she said with a sigh.

Celia turned down the lamp on the nightstand and climbed under the covers. I waited for a moment and then removed the last of my clothing and slowly approached the bed. I lifted the heavy satin quilt and eased my naked body down onto the cool sheets.

A foot roughly shoved me onto the floor.

"Say now!" I protested. "You can't expect me to spend the entire voyage sleeping on that torture rack of a couch! Why, a child could barely fit on it!"

Without turning, Celia spoke in her coolest, most even tones.

"As I made clear on the first night we met, Mr. Bowen, ours is strictly a *business* association. You freely agreed to my terms. Now you may help yourself to a pillow. But if you attempt anything more than that, you will again find yourself confronted by my gun. Pleasant dreams, darling."

CHAPTER 8

Nigel Bowen
Atlantic Ocean
Thursday, April 11, 1912, 3:30 PM

I WAS BEING FOLLOWED.

It was the oddest sensation, all the more unexpected for occurring within the confines of a ship, even one as large as the *Titanic*.

I was in a foul mood from a frustrating attempt at napping on that infernal couch. Since I needed my wits about me this evening, I thought it best to avoid the bar in the smoking room and have a good sweat in the Turkish baths as second-best relief.

But as I was ambling along one of the middle decks, I was suddenly overcome with the certainty that I was being observed. At first I thought it just lingering paranoia after my nerve-racking escape from Southampton. I casually glanced behind me but saw only a harried steward bustling one way and an exhausted laundress lumbering the other.

I slowed down as I came to a passage that was one story

above the squash court. I paused and looked down through
the viewing window. Below, Vogel was trying to teach his
son the proper way to hold a racket. Noticing me, they
both gave friendly waves. As I returned the greeting, I saw
in the reflection a large bald man just down the hall behind
me. He lingered for a moment and then, catching my gaze
in the glass, briskly turned and headed down a side passageway. I quickly followed in the direction he had gone.
The side passage was empty so I went up a deck and, seeing
another empty passage, went up the next flight of stairs. Finally, I came out onto the Boat Deck, the level on which
the lifeboats were kept; there weren't any in the restricted
first class area as they tended to block one's view of the
ocean.

There were a few passengers at the rail staring out to sea.
The bald man was standing with his back to me, noncha-
lantly smoking a cigar and chatting with an older steward.
I wondered if there was a way I could test my hunch that
he was tailing me beyond running wildly across the deck to
see if he followed.

Glancing around, I saw Emily Moore sitting in a deck
chair, reading. She was an auburn-haired young girl, pretty
if rather starchy; I wasn't sure if stiffness was her true nature or the result of her domineering father's influence. I
decided to find out—and see if Miss Moore could be of use
in testing my bald friend.

"And what are proper young ladies reading these days?" I said, startling her. "A rousing western or a dreary romance?"

Emily smiled sheepishly. "Oh! I'm afraid I'm not a very good example of a proper young lady...."

She held up her book to reveal a lurid detective novel, colorfully entitled *The Woman Stealer.* The crudely drawn cover showed a bound and gagged young woman being fought over by two men.

"I'm shocked!" I cried. "As I'm sure your father is by such sensational material."

Taking her arm, I firmly lifted her out of the chair.

"Let's give him even more to be outraged about," I said. "Take an unchaperoned turn about the ship with a married man."

"Well, I don't—" She tried to protest, but I had already pulled her in the opposite direction of Baldy. I led her down the passage I had just come out of. When we got to the first staircase, I glanced back. A waiter with a room service tray paused at the Boat Deck door and backed up to allow someone to come in. I hurried our pace down the stairs.

"Is this a stroll or a race, Mr. Bowen?" Emily asked, a bit breathlessly.

I quickly took her through another passage, then all but dragged her down a staircase at the far end. I looked back, but Baldy was nowhere in sight. A trio of officers passed by and, now wanting to stall, I stopped one of them.

"Officer, could you tell us where—er, the Boat Deck is?" I asked him.

"But we've just come from there!" Emily protested.

I looked down the hall and sure enough, Baldy was coming down the stairs; seeing me, he instantly doubled back. Whoever he was, he was terrible at masking his mission. I wondered if that was the point.

"Oh, of course!" I laughed. "I meant…oh, the squash court."

The officer looked at me queerly. "You're standing in front of it, sir."

I nodded my thanks and opened the door for Emily. She looked at me oddly and, as there was no one in the court, slowly entered it.

"I'm afraid I *really* don't understand you, Mr. Bowen."

Closing the door behind us, I looked up at the viewing window. Baldy was now one deck above looking down at us. He was one of those men who had a cruel look about him even when he was smiling, which he was doing. He bared his very white and very sharp-looking teeth and slowly nodded to me before casually strolling off. He had wanted to be seen, after all.

"Mr. *Bowen!*" Emily said in testy confusion, hands now

on hips. I couldn't blame her—my actions had probably made me look like a lunatic.

"Forgive me, Miss Moore, but…" I stuttered. "Well…I simply wanted a little alone time with you."

Emily looked at me with a stunned, wide-eyed expression—one that very quickly bloomed into a grin of delight.

"Oh, how romantic!" she gasped. She fell into my arms and pushed me up against the door. "Darling!" she murmured.

I felt I had little choice but to take her in my arms and kiss her deeply—all the while making sure we were flat against the wall beneath the viewing window so no one above could see us.

Emily sighed with excitement as I cooed into her ear, "Dear—*dearest!*"

Oh, and reaching into the folds of her voluminous skirt, I also lifted her expensively beaded bag.

CHAPTER 9

Nigel Bowen
Atlantic Ocean
Thursday, April 11, 1912, 5:30 PM

CELIA SLAPPED ME with such startling harshness it echoed in our tiny bathroom.

"My dear!" I cried. "That truly *hurt!* It's a fine day when a man can't show a little affection to his wife without being assaulted."

I rubbed my aching cheek in a feeble attempt at sympathy. Celia calmly put away her towel and lightly pushed past me out the bathroom door.

"I'm beginning to think you *like* it," she said over her shoulder. "But I'll review the terms of our arrangement as many times as you require: our marriage is just a front, and if you don't keep your hands to yourself, I'll plug you full of lead."

Smiling broadly, she began choosing her evening gown, all the while clutching her thin robe against her body. Though I'd never seen my "wife" undressed, the clinging silk left little to the imagination.

"You have strange notions of propriety," I observed as I dropped onto my couch/bed. "For a whore."

Celia's hairbrush missed my temple by a whisper and thumped loudly against the cabin wall; her throwing arm was clearly as able as her catching.

"I am *not* a whore," she said calmly. "That was a disguise I used to find a partner."

I held up my hands and pretended to cower in the couch.

"And a most convincing disguise at that." I smiled. "One wonders what could have driven you to such lengths."

"Well, I could hardly take out an advertisement." She sighed. "Listen, Nigel, picking pockets and winning at cards is all well and good, but some of the wealthiest and most prominent persons alive are aboard the *Titanic*. I want to set our sights on bigger game! Listen, if we—"

"Why do you get to plan everything?" I interrupted, annoyed. "Did it ever occur to you that I might have some thoughts about this operation?"

There was a knock at the door, and for a moment I thought it might be my bald friend paying a visit. But it was just a scullery maid bringing Celia fresh towels.

"Evening, Mr. Bjornstrom, sir," she said with a light curtsy.

As she entered the room, I suddenly noticed that

Emily's handbag and Phil's watch were sitting plainly out on the bureau—directly where the woman was headed! Not knowing how else to create a distraction, I reached out and pinched her bottom.

The maid whipped around in startled indignation and the towels went flying. Celia looked up in surprise at the commotion but quickly saw the items on the bureau. As the maid angrily bent to retrieve the towels, I took the moment to discreetly sweep the stolen goods into the top drawer.

The air was understandably strained, so I pulled out a few shillings and handed them to the woman. She took them with great reluctance—the same spirit in which they were offered, for she was most unattractive.

After she huffed out the door, I turned to Celia. "I hope your ambitious plans for bigger game include covering our tracks more carefully, my dear. That was an unforgivably sloppy oversight."

"Well, if you hadn't felt the need to make yet *another* pass at me, my attention might not have been diverted!" she retorted.

"Oh, all right." I sighed now with true irritation. "I resign my campaign of seduction; forgive me for being quite *swept* away by your mystery and beauty. As it is, I have other matters on my mind. I was followed today."

Celia gathered her robe and picked up a fresh towel.

"Who would follow you? One of your acquaintances from Southampton?"

I mulled over the suggestion. "Hmm, I wonder. He certainly wasn't one of my fellow card players, but it's possible they sent some mug on their behalf. Where is this fabled gun of yours, anyway?"

"Make another pass and it will appear in an instant!"

I threw my hands up. "Celia, I'm convinced you went to finishing school in a military barrack."

She laughed and reverted to her mock Cockney. "Oh, no, why, only the finest con-*tee*-nental salons for a fine lady like me-self, guv!"

She gave me a saucy wink and back kick as she opened the bathroom door, but her action caused her flimsy robe to slip off one shoulder. Against the porcelain skin of her back, two lengthy purple-red scars stood out so vividly it was as if the wounds had been inflicted that very morning.

She closed the door.

CHAPTER 10

Celia Bowen
Atlantic Ocean
Thursday, April 11, 1912, 7:30 PM

"THANK YOU FOR sharing your thoughts on the matter, Celia dear," Nigel said to me across the dining table, his words slurred. "But I'm told that in traditional marriages—which you never tire of reminding me that ours is *not*—the man does what he likes, when he likes."

The other diners watched silently as Nigel threw back the rest of the wine in his goblet and sloppily poured another—at least his fifth. "So we will proceed with *my* plan: a nice game of bridge with the stakes raised to celebrate our second night at sea!"

Nigel lifted his glass to me, then looked drunkenly around at the other gentlemen, who were clearly uncomfortable with his words and manner; the ladies were aghast. I gave Nigel a warning glance that he'd gone too far. He just stared back at me.

"I don't know what you are trying to communicate with that dire look, dear *wife*," he said in an ugly tone. "But as I'm sure you have other, more ambitious and grandiose plans for the evening, I suggest you get to them."

"See here, old man," Phil piped up with an angry red face. "Your tone is most objectionable. You've had enough for one night."

Nigel turned to him with a hostile glare. "Afraid to give me the chance to win back some of my money, *old man*? Or are you just grateful for the chance to rush to my wife's defense?"

I stood up as calmly as possible. The other ladies at the table turned and gave me sympathetic looks. I guessed there'd already been discussion about how much money Nigel had lost—now it would be about how disgraceful his manner was. And after the glances the ladies had been giving their husbands, I doubted Nigel would be able to initiate the smoking of cigars, let alone a card game.

"If you'll excuse me," I said to all, "I feel a slight headache…"

Surprisingly, old man Davies beat Phil to his feet.

"Do me the honor of letting me escort you, Mrs. Bowen," he said, giving me an earnest look. "As you've already seen, there are disreputable characters all over this ship."

"Is that quip directed at me, *older* man?" Nigel snarled.

"You foremost, among others," Davies said with quiet dignity as he gently took my arm. As he guided me away from the table, I overheard Nigel say, "Tough luck, Phil. The bigger bank account always wins. With her anyway."

Davies and I stopped in the lobby of the luxurious À la Carte Restaurant and he waved a bill at the attendant for my wrap. He then said, "Perhaps a short walk would make you—well, might put a more soothing end to the evening?"

I nodded and we walked slowly out onto the deck. Davies cleared his throat, then paused and pressed a hand to his stomach. He seemed in pain, but upon seeing my wondering look, he brushed it off.

"Just some indigestion. I must say, your husband's coarse behavior makes me feel that much more ashamed about my own toward you this morning." He sighed regretfully. "A man of my class gets to be my age and, well, he thinks the world and anything in it is his for the taking—or at least he tries to convince himself that it is. I hope you can forgive me."

"It's already forgotten, Mr. Davies," I said with a smile. "But I'll always remember your kindness this evening."

We continued our walk for some time, at least an hour. Like so many successful and long-married men, Davies was desperately lonely. At first he tried to explain how the unhappiness of his marriage had influenced his advances toward me. But soon the many aspects of the *Titanic* grabbed his attention, as it did apparently *all* the men onboard. He excitedly pointed out that the vessel was the largest man-made moving object ever built, it had cost well over seven million dollars, there were over two thousand passengers aboard, and the ship had twenty lifeboats.

At last we came to the passage containing my cabin. Startled, Davies brought himself up short.

"Good lord, I've talked your ear off!" he exclaimed outside my door. "It is *you,* Mrs. Bowen, who have shown the greater kindness tonight by indulging me."

"Don't be silly. I enjoyed our walk tremendously!" I insisted. "It took my mind off…"

I let my words sadly trail away and Davies looked at me with what seemed genuine concern. He waited while I entered and flicked on the light. I turned to him and held out my hand.

"All marriages have their troubles, Mr. Davies," I said with a smile of resignation. "Whether a marriage of thirty years or three days.…"

He took my hand and brought it to his lips and kissed it for a full ten seconds. As he looked up, I was astonished to see tears in his eyes.

I covered his hand with mine and gently smiled. Davies paused, then pulled my body against his. I looked up at him with astonishment.

"You wonderful, *beautiful* woman…" He sighed.

I had just started to push him away when someone staggered into the room with a grunt. Davies turned around and gasped at the sight of Nigel, who was disheveled and clearly even drunker than before.

"Well, I seem to be throwing off all your plans tonight, *dearest,*" he sneered. "Here's another curveball: look what I found."

He reached into his open jacket.

And pulled out my gun.

CHAPTER 11

Celia Bowen
Atlantic Ocean
Thursday, April 11, 1912, 9:45 PM

DAVIES STEPPED IN front of me, protecting me with his body.

"Bowen! Don't be a damned fool, put that gun away!" he hissed.

Grinning drunkenly, Nigel brought the gun up to his eye level and playfully aimed at the older man.

"Would be quite a scandal, eh?" Nigel taunted. "Blue blood shot after making love to woman of questionable background aboard world's most famous ship. Pretty headlines for your wife and daughters to read, eh?"

Davies drew his body up to full height. "How dare you threaten me with blackmail! Have you no decency?"

Nigel stumbled and fell onto my bed—all without taking the gun off Davies. "You're not in the best position to lecture on decorum, Mr. D; not with your hands full of my wife."

I stepped out from behind Davies.

"Nigel, put that gun down," I begged him. "What madncss has gotten into you? What will the other passengers think of you—of *us?*"

Nigel's smirk dropped. "I can tell you what they think of *me,* darling. I'm a cad who can't hold his liquor, a swine who doesn't appreciate his beautiful wife, and...a broke bugger who just lost every cent they had on this ship."

"Nigel, no!" I cried as my hand flew up to my mouth. "What will we *do?*"

He sat up and, tossing the gun across the bed, buried his face in his hands. Davies stared at him, then quietly walked over to the door and closed it.

"You must let me help you, my dear," he said gravely.

I stifled a sob. "There's nothing you or anyone can do, Mr. Davies. Our reputations are as ruined as our fortunes. If only there were some way we could get off this wretched ship!"

I burst into tears and turned away from him. I heard him approach Nigel.

"Listen here, Bowen," he commanded. I looked back and Nigel slowly lifted his head. His eyes were bleary and unfocused.

"We've both of us acted disgracefully toward your wife," he said in the stern tones of a politician. "But we both can and *will* make amends."

Davies sat down at the writing desk and pulled out his checkbook.

"I am writing an amount here that should cover your losses and provide comfortably for you and your wife for some time to come," Davies said as he briskly wrote. "That is what I am going to do."

He held the check out. Nigel looked at it as if it were dead vermin.

"What *you* are going to do," Davies barked, "is accept this amount with the promise that you will *never* gamble again or in any way threaten your wife—or anyone else, for that matter. If you do, I care nothing of the scandal, I will do everything in my power to help her divorce you."

Nigel looked guiltily over at me, then squared his shoulders and stood up—though he wavered with the roll of the ship.

"That was quite a speech, *sir*," Nigel hissed. "You asked me if I have any decency. Well, what decent, self-respecting man would accept such a handout—especially from the man he caught making love to his wife?"

"Nigel, please," I beseeched him. "Accept Mr. Davies's extraordinary offer. It's our only hope! Please, for *me!*"

Nigel paused, then slowly reached out and took the check from Davies's hand. He didn't look at it, just walked over to me and placed it in my hand.

"I don't see how I will ever be able look you in eye again." He sighed miserably and, turning away, lay down again on the bed.

Davies cleared his throat and put his hand on the door-knob. "I will say goodnight now. I trust this evening will look different to all of us in the morning."

He gave me a reassuring nod and closed the door after him. I looked down at the check. It was for a *fortune*. I slowly walked over to Nigel, who had an arm thrown over his face.

"It's a great deal of money," I said. "But…it's still not enough to buy you access to my bed. So shove off."

Nigel peeked out from under his arm and we both burst out laughing. He leapt up and took my arms.

"We *did* it!" he cried, though I tried to shush him. He swung me around the room and I was so giddy with the success of our venture that I let him.

"The beautiful thing is that Davies doesn't even *know* he was just extorted!" I laughed. "In fact, in handing over an enormous sum of money, he thinks he's taken the high ground!"

"Well, of course! He's single-handedly saved our marriage!" Nigel exclaimed. He continued to whirl me around until we were both quite out of breath. We laughingly slumped together down on the bed. I lifted a warning finger.

"There is a cost, though, Nigel. A steep one for you," I said. "You can't gamble the rest of the voyage."

"Good god! What will I do with myself?" he gasped.

"It also occurs to me that everyone *hates* me now! I'm not used to being unpopular."

"Then you can spend the rest of the passage working to redeem your rotten character," I said as I got up and began undressing for the night. "Nothing delights ladies more than being in the position of granting forgiveness."

Nigel reached out a hand. "We make quite a team—don't we, old girl?"

"Success doesn't alter our terms," I reminded him. "But I will admit it's rather fun pretending to be married to you, Mr. Bowen."

I gave his hand a warm little squeeze. He tried to hold on but I pulled away with a gentle slap.

"It's just too bad that the rest of the voyage is going to be so dull."

CHAPTER 12

Nigel Bowen
Atlantic Ocean
Friday, April 12, 1912, 9:00 AM

CELIA STIRRED IN my arms as I gently stroked her fleecy golden hair. She pulled away slightly so I softly drew her nearer. She then pushed her pelvis against mine but not in a sensual way; she did it to move away from me. I firmly turned her over on her back, and her eyes flew open, startled. As I went in to kiss her, she began laughing—a harsh, awful, enraging laugh. And the laughter somehow got stronger...even as my hands went around her throat.

I woke surprisingly slowly—so slowly that I was aware that I was dreaming before Celia's face began to fade. But her laughter—and that knowing smile—lingered as I opened my eyes and found myself alone in the empty cabin.

Good God, Nigel! I gasped to myself as I sat up. I found myself yet again on the cramped couch—sheets, blankets, and clothes strewn all around me. Across the room, the bed was neatly made and Celia's possessions were tidily in place on the nightstand. Phil's watch told me it was after nine in the morning.

My disturbing dream made me uneasy about not knowing where Celia was. As I hurriedly dressed, I tried to reassure myself that all was well: Celia had proved a most resourceful accomplice, and our Davies scheme had been wildly successful. All we had to do now was protect our cover and wait out the rest of the trip.

I guessed our group would be gathered after breakfast on the covered Promenade Deck and, indeed, as I entered the warm enclosure I immediately spotted Mrs. Sedgwick, Mrs. Minahan, and the Vogels. At the far end, Celia and Phil were tossing a ball with little Arthur. I breezed in with my usual cheery smile but quickly recalled that I was a social outcast and adjusted my expression.

"Good morning," I said to the group as solemnly as possible. "I'm utterly ashamed of my behavior last night. I've sworn to Celia that I won't take another drink nor lift another card. And I hope for the chance to make amends to each and every one of you."

Everyone looked uneasily to Mrs. Sedgwick for the "official" group response. She peered at me down her long nose. "Your words are commendable, Mr. Bowen, but it will be your actions over the duration of the voyage and beyond that will prove your worthiness."

I nodded my head abashedly—biting back the impulse

to tell the old busybody to stuff it up her bloody rear. With a tip of my hat I made my way down the deck to where Celia and Phil were romping with Arthur. Celia's back was to me, and Phil was too enraptured with her presence to note my own. Celia suddenly threw her head back and rocked with laughter at something the child had done— and placed her hand on Phil's chest to steady herself. Phil covered her hand with his—and left it there.

I felt my face go hot with a blood rush of anger.

My anger was partially with Celia for continuing her flirtatious ways and partially with Phil for treating me like a chump. But mostly my anger was with myself. For in that terrible instant, I realized I had fallen in love with Celia.

Unable to stop myself, I lunged forward and confronted the two.

"Kindly take your hands off of my wife, Mr. Colley," I said through gritted teeth.

Celia's eyes flashed toward mine with a look of both alarm and caution.

"Oh, Nigel!" She a forced little laugh. "Don't tell me you've *already* fallen back on your word and started the day with spirits!"

Celia's eyes implored me to play along, to use her cue to make it all a joke, to not blow the cover we desperately needed to keep. I knew what I should do, yet I couldn't help myself.

"I don't need to be drunk to defend my wife's honor—or my own!" I said indignantly. Phil jutted his chin out and clenched his fists but Celia intervened and, grabbing my arm, pulled me away to the promenade window.

"What on earth are you *doing?*" she hissed.

"You've already taken that boy for all that he had," I said testily. "Why continue to throw yourself at him?"

"Have you gone *mad?* You're risking everything we've gained!" she cried. "Davies could wire his bank and cancel that check *at any time!*"

"That's all that matters to you, isn't it—*the money?*" I demanded, then tried to soften my tone. "Celia—darling—"

"Of course the money is all that matters!" she fumed. "Nigel, I risked *everything* on this scheme, and now that I've gotten what I wanted I refuse to lose it because of your childish, possessive whims. Why, you make a boy like Phil seem ten times the man you are!"

I went to reach for her, but it must have looked as if I were going to strike, as Phil suddenly stepped up and twisted my arm around so that I faced him. Being part of Yale's rowing crew had given him the advantage of strength, but I had fury on my side so we tussled equally for a moment. Each of us got in one good hit—me to Phil's gut, him to my jaw—before Vogel stepped between us.

"Gentlemen! Stop this at once!" he barked with surprising force for such a bookish-looking man. Celia backed away up against the deck window, her eyes shut and her hand clasped over her mouth. Seeing her distress, old Sedgwick sailed forward and took her gently by the arm.

"Come, my dear," she said quietly but with iron firmness. "Come to my cabin and collect yourself. There you can shield yourself from not only Mr. Bowen's latest display of boorishness but also the gossip it will inspire. Though I am afraid it will only be a temporary refuge from both...."

CHAPTER 13

Celia Bowen
Atlantic Ocean
Friday, April 12, 1912, 10:30 AM

MRS. SEDGWICK'S FIRST class suite made my cabin look like servants' quarters. The carved-wood furniture and wain-scoting were much the same, but everything seemed on a larger scale and her accommodations featured a cozy sitting room. Mrs. Sedgwick graciously welcomed me in and curtly instructed her maid, Kitty—a fresh-faced but terrified-looking young Irish lass—to serve tea.

As Kitty nervously poured, I looked around the room and noted the array of framed photographs that Mrs. Sedgwick had propped up around the place—clearly all members of her eminent family. Fathers, mothers, daughters, sons, nieces—it seemed her entire family tree was represented. However, the dress and manner of the pictures indicated times well gone by, and I couldn't help but notice how scuffed some of the glass panes were. Looking closer, I saw that many of the ornate frames were chipped and scratched.

"You must go on a great many voyages, Mrs. Sedgwick," I observed.

She looked up from her teacup. "Why do you say that, my dear?"

"Oh! It's just that your photographs...they look so—so well traveled!" I stumbled, hoping to make it sound like a lark instead of implied criticism.

"Until this passage I have not sailed or traveled in any capacity in nearly twenty years," Mrs. Sedgwick said heavily. "Business took me to London. Unfortunate financial dealings related to my family. Our situation is, in fact, well illustrated by those photographs: once quite grand but now...rather shabby."

She looked sadly down into her teacup. I wasn't quite sure what she was telling me. I again looked around the room with its silken curtains and plush sofas and loveseats. Mrs. Sedgwick saw my glance and gave a wan smile.

"Yes, the Sedgwick name ensures that I am able to reside in one of the finest suites on the ship." She nodded. "But it's all on credit. To be quite frank, dear Celia, though we have properties and holdings all over Manhattan, I'm afraid we are what is termed 'cash poor.'"

I made a sympathetic murmur, then took refuge in my teacup. I was at a complete loss as to how I was to react to such a bold and intimate disclosure.

"How unforgivable of me!" Mrs. Sedgwick suddenly gasped. "I asked you here to cheer you and all I've done is bore you with my own troubles. But I shall redeem myself!"

She excitedly put down her tea and busily made her way across the room. Shifting through some books and papers on a sideboard, she pulled out a sheaf of cheap-looking magazines. Grinning like a bold schoolgirl about to smoke her first cigarette, the older woman sat down next to me on the settee and placed the publications on her knees. I recognized them immediately as police gazettes, tabloids that reported all the salacious details of the most sensational crimes of the day. They often included crime scene drawings and photographs.

"I'm afraid I became quite a fan of your British magazines while in London. I confess that I hide them from Kitty, as it's quite unseemly for a woman of my station to take interest in such low material!" She giggled. "But I do find them an effective distraction from my woes."

She gleefully flipped through a few issues and pointed out several reports of especially lurid and gruesome crimes, evidently her favorites. I didn't know if I was expected to gasp in horror or pretend to share her delight, so I said nothing.

Finally, she picked up the last issue from the stack and flipped to an article that had been flagged with a bookmark. She shifted in her seat so that she was even closer to me and turned the magazine fully to my view.

"Here's what I really wanted to show you!" she said. I looked down at the yellowy, cheaply printed page and

read the headline PRETTY PICKPOCKET PREYS ON PIC-
CADILLY! I ran my eyes over the article detailing the ex-
ploits of an "exceptionally beautiful blond lass" who was
currently being sought as the prime suspect in a string of
robberies, all involving male members of the upper class.

I slowly turned to look at Mrs. Sedgwick. She was staring at me expectantly.

"Extraordinary, isn't it?" she asked.

"I'm not sure I know what you mean...," I said evenly.

Sedgwick snorted with amusement, then pointed at the
mug shot at the bottom of the page.

"The *likeness,* my dear!" she exclaimed breathlessly.
"Why you're the *spitting image* of this naughty 'Molly
Mitchell'!"

I looked down at the stark photograph of the wide-
eyed, defiant-looking woman. I stared at it for some time,
wordlessly. When I finally looked up, Mrs. Sedgwick had
that same expectant look on her face—but this time her
meaning was quite clear.

I slowly picked up my bag. I reached in and pulled out
several bills—large ones. I silently placed them on the table, where they sat between us for several seconds. Mrs.
Sedgwick then scooped them up in one effortless quick
movement, and they vanished into the folds of her dress.

"That will do quite nicely, my dear," she said with a
bright smile. "For now. Another cup of tea?"

CHAPTER 14

Nigel Bowen
Atlantic Ocean
Friday, April 12, 1912, 11:00 AM

MY MIND WAS spinning as I walked at top speed around the deck; I lost track of how many laps I did. I was vaguely aware of curious stares from the other passengers, but I didn't care. They probably thought me mad or—more likely—drunk, but walking was the only way I could focus on the problems I'd created earlier.

If he hadn't heard already, it was only a matter of time before Davies learned that I'd publicly fought with Celia and come to blows with Phil. The most likely scenario was that since I clearly had not turned over a new leaf after all, he'd cancel the check and offer to help Celia divorce me—only to eventually learn that we weren't even married. Yes, I'd mucked this one up good.

Despite my preoccupied thoughts, I eventually became aware of that feeling again—the certainty that I was being followed. I whipped around and tried to spot my bald friend through the throngs of people on the deck. Aware that he was probably wearing a hat for the deck, I slowed my pace and, at the last minute, dove into the small alcove next to the Marconi wireless office. Several passengers and officers passed me without notice until one person came hurrying along, whipping her head back in forth as though frantically searching for something.

Emily Moore.

When I sighed loudly she turned my way and badly feigned surprise at seeing me.

"Oh! Fancy running into *you*, Nigel!" she exclaimed, hand on chest.

"Astonishing, Miss Moore," I said with a slight bow.

She gave a little pout and playfully pushed my arm. "Why so formal and distant? And furthermore, why haven't you made *any* effort to see me since…well, you *know!*"

She giggled girlishly as I walked her back onto the open deck.

"Darling," she said excitedly, "can you take me back to that tennis court or whatever it was? I seem to have dropped an awfully expensive bag somewhere near there. Father will have a stroke if he finds out I lost it. It belonged to mother."

Seeing no way out, I absently nodded and escorted her down a flight of stairs that would eventually lead us to G Deck, just above the ship's waterline.

"Did you *really* strike your wife this morning?" she inquired excitedly. "The whole ship seems to be talking about it. I hope the row wasn't about *me!*"

"Good lord, don't be daft," I said rather irritably.

"Daft about *me* being the cause or about *you* striking Mrs. Bowen?"

I halted our walk. "I did *not* strike my wife this morning or any other morning, Miss Moore. We simply had an argument—the kind married people have all the time. Mr. Colley misinterpreted what he saw, and that, well, that led to the talk that is apparently flying about this damned ship."

Emily frowned. "You're in a mood. I daresay I believe all this talk about your violent nature. I half expect you to fling me to the court floor and savagely thrash me."

"You probably deserve it," I said, sensing the idea thrilled her.

We reached the squash court and saw that it was currently occupied.

"Well, we can't search the court now," I observed. "Surely if the bag has been found it's been turned in to an officer or some sort of Lost and Found department."

"Oh, I don't care about the blasted bag...." Emily sighed with disappointment. Clearly she had hoped for a replay of our little intimacy. I started back toward the main flight of stairs. She followed reluctantly and then, spying a sort of closet area underneath the steps, yanked me in that direction. She grasped my lapels and tried to pull me in for a kiss.

I gently took her wrists. "Miss Moore…I'm very sorry I let myself get carried away by…well, your charm and youth the other day. But, you see, the sad fact of the matter is that I am truly and most desperately in love with Celia."

I had hoped my unadorned honesty would earn me some points, but tears sprang immediately to her eyes. "Oh, you're *awful!* You're just as much of a cad as everyone says you are!"

I accepted the accusation with a resigned nod. She stamped her foot and, reaching up, loudly slapped me.

The sound echoed down the quiet corridor then mingled with the sounds of steps moving down the staircase. At the base, there arrived absolutely the two last people I would have hoped to see at that particular moment: Emily's father, Mr. Langston Moore, and—inevitably, given my luck this day—Mr. Randolph Davies.

CHAPTER 15

Celia Bowen
Atlantic Ocean
Friday, April 12, 1912, 12:30 PM

HOW MUCH WOULD she expect? I asked myself, over and over. *How would I get it before we docked? And how on earth would I be able to hide it from Nigel?*

I had left Mrs. Sedgwick's cabin at least an hour earlier and had been standing at the ship's railing ever since. I stared out at the Atlantic as it slowly seemed to grow as dark and turbulent as my mood. A breeze blew in, so I moved closer to a bulkhead that separated one part of the deck from another. I hadn't meant to hide, but apparently I couldn't be seen, as several moments later I heard some ladies' voices approach and immediately recognized the nasal twang of Mrs. Minahan.

"She puts on a good act, I'll give her that," she was saying. "But she gives herself away every time Mr. Colley is around. She practically threw herself in his arms this morning the moment her husband showed up. She seems to enjoy goading him."

"Mr. Bowen is so handsome!" another woman gushed.

"I suppose she's pretty enough in a cheap sort of way, but I think he could do much better."

"Setting your sights, Ethel?" Mrs. Minahan sarcastically asked. The other ladies laughed. "I wouldn't be at all surprised if they divorce."

"You don't mean it!" another woman exclaimed. "Think of the scandal!"

"Oh, I doubt scandal matters much to them. They don't seem to have *any* social connections," Mrs. Minahan droned on. "The fact is that while Mr. Bowen can be charming, he's a terrible drunk. For all we know, *she* is too. She wears lipstick, you know. I'm dead certain she's a gold digger. I suggest for the duration of the voyage we keep as far away from them as possible."

At that, I took two steps forward, which put me directly in the middle of the deck. Several of the ladies audibly gasped at my sudden appearance. I looked Mrs. Minahan directly in the face.

"Mrs. Bowen!" she exclaimed with an embarrassed bark. She quickly cleared her throat. "We didn't realize you were there, obviously. I'm afraid you caught us doing the one thing ladies always seem to do when we're away from the men!"

She gave a nervous little laugh, which one or two of the others joined in halfhearted support.

"Yes." I nodded. "I've often wondered if idle gossip was

the reason the men are always so eager to separate themselves from the women after dinner. You've rather settled my mind on the matter."

The ladies gaped at one another in astonished outrage. I took the moment to dig into my bag and pulled out a cigarette. I stared at them as I slowly lit it.

"You seem to want to keep clear of me. Let me help you on your way," I said, and then exhaled a strong stream of smoke directly at their faces. Hands and handkerchiefs flew to delicate nostrils.

Mrs. Minahan stared at the cigarette in shocked horror. "And *you,* Mrs. Bowen, have rather proven *my* point!"

She quickly gathered her cronies and hurriedly led them away toward the first class grand staircase. I watched them go for a moment, then turned and flicked the cigarette overboard. I realized that alienating possible allies was a silly thing to do, but I had to admit to myself that it had felt good—*very* good.

Having no other option, I followed down the deck after them. Sooner or later, I'd have to return to the cabin and have it out with Nigel. I supposed I might as well get it over with.

But only two or three steps farther, the prospect of another argument was too much for me and, spying a snug-looking deck chair half hidden under a lifeboat, I flung myself down on it. I closed my eyes and let my body rise and fall with the steady roll of the ship. I almost wished I could spend the rest of the voyage floating out alone in the chilly sea—away from Mrs. Sedgwick and her demands, away from people and their prying, away from pretending and lying and stealing. I was feeling very tired of it all.

I thought about digging out another cigarette—one I could really enjoy this time instead of wasting it as a prop—and was just about to do so, when I heard something stir behind me. I started to turn around, but suddenly a rough hand clapped over my mouth and another reached under my chest. Before I could react or register in any way to what was happening, I was lifted and dragged into a darkened corridor.

CHAPTER 16

Nigel Bowen
Atlantic Ocean
Friday, April 12, 1912, 1:00 PM

I MOST DEFINITELY needed a drink.

But was I still bound to my vow of sobriety? Old man Davies had given me a very pointed *dis*appointed stare at the bottom of the stairs but had said nothing. He had simply walked away as Mr. Moore dressed down Emily for being alone with a married man. How could Davies now see me as anything but a violence-prone bully who seduced chaste young ladies? What was the point of pretending I wasn't drinking if I'd *again* proven myself unworthy of my wife?

I decisively headed in the direction of the smoking lounge. But as I came up the Grand Staircase, Fate seemed to caution me—by throwing a large rubber ball directly into my crotch. I gasped and, automatically grabbing the ball, looked up to see little Arthur Vogel running toward me. Life on the ship seemed to agree with the boy. He no longer had the worried, serious look of the first day out. His cheeks were now flushed, and his mop of yellow hair flopped as he happily jumped up and down and indicated for me to toss the ball back to him.

I obliged and then looked up to see Mr. and Mrs. Vogel at the top of the landing; they exchanged a worried frown between them. Association with me was clearly not something they wanted for their child.

I nodded politely to the couple and, patting Arthur good-naturedly on the head, I passed him on the stairs and went out onto the deck.

But the boy wanted to play. I soon heard him tottering after me, calling, "Mister! Mister!" I turned and he again tossed the ball to me. I had no choice but to catch it and throw it back. This time Mrs. Vogel trotted out onto the deck after her son and, brusquely taking his arm, deliberately turned him away from me. They joined Mr. Vogel, who had stopped to join a small clutch of young couples that were pointing to something out at sea.

I continued along and, sure enough, the ball came bouncing past me. I pretended not to notice it until I heard the patter of feet coming up behind me. I turned to see Arthur bounding after his ball—which was headed toward a narrow stairway down to the next deck. Arthur heedlessly ran directly into it.

Without thinking, I threw myself in front of the child. I was able to stop his flight, but in doing so, I had to slam my shoulder into an iron railing. Arthur's added weight increased the impact, and I completely lost my balance. Together, we both tumbled down the opening onto the deck below.

We landed with a loud *thud*—me on my back with Arthur gripped to my chest. The wind was almost completely knocked out of me, but in my concern for the child I sprang up and turned him around to face me.

"Again! Again!" the boy ecstatically cried. "Let's do it *again!*"

A distraught Mr. Vogel appeared at the top of the deck.

"Mr. Bowen! Is he all right?" he cried.

Arthur turned to look up at his father and excitedly waved. A young crew member hurried over and helped me up as Mr. Vogel came down the stairs and then guided his wife down. She pulled Arthur into her arms, squeezed him tightly, then took him by the shoulders. "That was very naughty, Arthur! You could have been most seriously *hurt!*"

Mrs. Vogel sprang to her feet and looked at me with nearly hysterical wide eyes. "Mr. Bowen—I can't—I don't even know how to—"

She burst into sobs. Her husband put his arm around her shoulders and held out his hand to me. "Mr. Bowen, we cannot thank you enough for your brave, selfless act. And all for the sake of a couple who have shown you little friendliness."

I shook my head and took Mr. Vogel's hand. "I haven't given you much reason to. And I can't accept compliments of bravery, as anyone in my position would have done the same. It was an almost completely automatic response."

"Which says much about your character," Mr. Vogel said gravely. "More than I had guessed. Please let us repay you in some way. At the very least, we would be delighted for you and Mrs. Bowen to be our guests for dinner. If I may say so, I think it is a gesture that your wife might appreciate, considering…recent difficulties."

He gave me a sharp look but one full of genuine compassion.

"Yes, yes, I see what you mean," I replied. "It would be an honor for us to join you."

We made plans for Sunday evening amid Mrs. Vogel repeatedly interrupting to ask if I needed to see the ship's doctor.

Once they left, I decided I'd earned if not a stiff drink then at least a good cigar. I took one out of my coat pocket and, lighting it, stared out at the vast ocean. It seemed a strangely lonely sight this particular afternoon—miles and miles of a dark blue broken only by the occasional white crest of a far-off wave.

As I inhaled the fine, rich smoke, the serene stillness was broken by a ghastly, blood-curdling scream.

I immediately recognized it as Celia's.

CHAPTER 17

Nigel Bowen
Atlantic Ocean
Friday, April 12, 1912, 1:30 PM

IN THE SHORT time I'd known her, I had seen Celia display many moods and emotions: anger, humor, disdain, passion. But I'd never seen her afraid.

Until now.

I had followed where I believed the scream to originate—somewhere behind the Bridge. The area was shadowy and strangely deserted. I paused for a moment—uncertain of which way to turn—and then heard a violent scuffling. I ran down a short, dark corridor and saw Celia pressed up against an exterior wall. Her expression was one of white shock. A dark, hulking figure was clutching both sides of her face. He roughly kissed her, but then, just as I started toward them, he viciously struck her.

I lunged at his back and momentarily locked eyes with Celia. If anything, my appearance seemed to strangely increase her distress. She shook her head at me but it was too late—I had already grasped the man's shirt cuff, and I hurled him to the floor. Within the space of a few seconds I was able to register that he was a swarthy, rough-looking man with curly hair. He was the type with a savage sexual quality that I knew some women found exciting. Absurdly—considering the circumstances—I thought of Emily Moore. This brute would appeal to her romantic notions of danger—and to her obvious desire to spit on the respectability her father demanded.

The enraged man jumped up from the floor and dove into me. Celia shrieked as her attacker and I punched, kicked, and tore at each other. Almost immediately, I heard the sound of pounding feet. Two officers in crisp white uniforms shoved their way into the scuffle and broke it apart. Somewhere in the back of my mind I registered that this was, incredibly, the *second* fistfight I'd been involved in that day!

Exhausted, I fell back against the wall and watched as the officers wrangled the muscular assailant to the ground. He was clad in a worker's soiled garments and had clearly not bathed or shaved in days. As he was subdued, he furiously flashed a glance at me with almost disturbingly bright hazel-green eyes.

"This man attacked my wife!" I choked out. "It's a miracle I came upon the scene in time to stop him."

The officers shook the wretch. "How'd you get from steerage up to first class?"

The man scowled and spat out, *"Va au diable!"*

I don't speak French but his meaning was clear to all.

"Throw him into whatever confinement you have!" I all but shouted. "Or better yet, toss him overboard!"

"No! *Please*—let him go! It was all a terrible misunderstanding!"

All heads turned in amazement to Celia. Though she still looked shaken to the core, she made a heroic effort to tamp down her true feelings and plastered on a blasé smile.

"It's all so—well—so very *silly!*" she exclaimed. "A simple language barrier. I don't want the poor man prosecuted because I couldn't understand what he was asking. I believe that he—well, he was lost and wanted only to return to the steerage area."

I gaped at Celia. "Darling, that's absolutely ridiculous. Why, I saw this man deliberately strike you! Why on *earth* are you defending him? You have nothing to fear—the officers will see that he is confined for the rest of the voyage."

Celia stepped forward without taking her eyes off mine. She put her hand on my arm and applied a pressure—unseen by the others—that was almost painful.

"Nigel, dear, it truly was all *my* fault," she said urgently. "I foolishly screamed when he—he accidentally startled me. He did not strike me—I simply lost my balance for a moment when the ship rolled. I insist that this man be let go. Immediately."

I looked into Celia's eyes with searching confusion; I

couldn't make her out for the life of me. The officers exchanged glances. They obviously regarded this as a very queer affair—and one they were reluctant to dismiss.

"Well, there's still the matter of his trespassing in first class, ma'am," one officer remarked. "We can't turn a blind eye to that. Order on the *Titanic* or any liner this size depends upon passengers' strict observance of class distinctions—in terms of the decks, of course."

Celia turned to the officer. I noticed that she had completely avoided looking at the Frenchman during the conversation. "But this gentlemen doesn't seem to speak English and, well, it is a huge and often confusing ship; I've gotten lost several times myself!"

"But, Celia, he had to climb six or seven decks *up* to get here!" I protested.

The officers had clearly had enough of this discussion.

"We'll have to detain him, ma'am," the officer insisted. "I'm sorry you were disturbed. If you change your mind about filing a complaint, do let us know."

With each holding one of the thug's arms, the officers began leading the assailant away. He didn't resist—in fact, he looked over and gave me a triumphant kind of *smile*.

But that wasn't even the strangest thing he did. He then turned to Celia and with an arched eyebrow muttered, *"Au revoir pour le moment…Molly."*

CHAPTER 18

Nigel Bowen
Atlantic Ocean
Friday, April 12, 1912, 2:00PM

ON THE WAY back to our cabin, neither of us said a word. But I watched Celia out of the corner of my eye, and I could all but see the wheels turning in her mind, faster than a locomotive. Whatever she was hiding, she was furiously working out how she could continue to do so.

Inside the room, Celia walked over to my bureau and poured a drink—the first I'd ever seen her take. She took a large sip then glanced over at me.

"Nigel, I think…" she said slowly, carefully. "I think we should separate. Everyone is talking about our argument and the fight you had with Phil. If you were to take another room, we might still be able to convince Mr. Davies that by a friendly separation we are striving to save our marriage."

I sat on the couch and contemplated her. She slowly paced back and forth across the room, her mind obviously still abuzz.

"You might even go to him and ask him to help you conquer your need for liquor," she said. "It would make him feel important. And it would seem as though you were *really* trying."

"And then what?" I asked tartly. "We dock, you decide that I truly *am* incorrigible and throw yourself into Davies's protective arms? Then you cash the check and disappear forever?"

Celia's eyes flashed with anger, but she made yet another effort to control herself. She walked over and sat next to me on the sofa.

"I haven't always been honest with you, Nigel," she said intently. "But I ask that you trust me this last time. You can have the money—all of it. It doesn't matter to me. Just please, *please* do as I say and take another room."

I laughed bitterly. "Not three hours ago you said the money was *all* that mattered to you. Come, my dear, you might start this new era of honesty by telling me who that Frenchman is. And who *you* are... Molly."

Celia sprang up from the sofa and went to her vanity. She stood with her back to me for several moments. She then suddenly dug into a drawer and, riffling through some papers, pulled something out. She walked up to me and held out Davies's check. "If I tell you about that man, will you promise—*swear*—to take this check and book another room?"

"Celia, darling, you're not very good at this kind of bargaining." I sighed in exasperation. "You must know that check is worthless if we part. I have no doubt that Davies will honor his word about helping you divorce me—until he finds out that there can be no divorce because there never was a marriage. You won't get a dime. You might even land in jail."

Her shoulders slumped, and it was as though I could actually see her fighting spirit rise out and float away. She sank down onto the couch again and pressed her head against the back. In a flat, dead kind of voice she spoke.

"His name is Gerard Remy. I met him when I was young…terribly young. He charmed me and loved me—or, what I supposed was love. And he introduced me to a wonderfully easy way to make money: pickpocketing. He trained me tirelessly. And I became very good at it."

She stopped for a moment and took another large drink. "But the better I became at theft, the more he seemed to resent it. He accused me of hiding money from him, of sleeping with the men I stole from. His jealousy grew and grew until he wouldn't allow me to leave our flat alone. He wouldn't let me out of his sight, so I couldn't work and so we fought about money. And then—then he began beating me."

I watched her carefully. Was she telling the truth or spinning a tale for some ulterior motive?

"I was so desperate to get away from him, I let myself be caught by the police. I felt I had a better chance of surviving prison than continuing with Gerard," she said with a tremble in her voice. "But he had connections and I was released—into *his* custody. The beating he gave me that time...I—I nearly died."

"But surely there must have been someone—"

She held her hand up weakly. "One night a few weeks ago I finally managed to escape him. But running from him was almost worse than being his prisoner. I knew he would be coming after me. I knew I *had* to get out of England. And I knew it would be far harder to trace me if I were part of a couple—if I had a partner, if I were a married woman. So I found you. And I thought it a great stroke of double luck when you so strangely insisted on adopting the Bjorn-stroms' name. I thought that ensured that I was completely untraceable.

"But, as you see, it didn't." She sighed. "He found me anyway..."

She closed her eyes and I could see her make an effort not to cry.

"But just now you had the chance to put the brute away!" I protested. "Why didn't you press charges?"

Celia gave a half laugh and shook her head helplessly. We sat quietly for a few moments, and, given her turmoil, I wondered if she had fallen asleep. Suddenly there was a light knocking on the door. I quietly got up and crossed the room. But just as I began to open the door, Celia seemed to come around. She sprang up and cried, "No! *Don't* open it, Nigel!"

But the door was already open. I looked outside and there was Baldy. Before I could say a word, he smashed a fist across my mouth.

My head rocked backward, but instinctively I flung my fist out and connected with the side of his head—but he crashed a great paw into my stomach and I reeled back onto the floor.

"Next time you poke your nose where it ought not to be, chum," he said in a surprisingly clipped accent, "right over the rail you'll go—into the drink."

He spat down at me, turned, and left.

As I lay there dazed, all I could think to myself was: "And that makes fistfight number *three...*"

CHAPTER 19

Nigel Bowen
Atlantic Ocean
Friday, April 12, 1912, 3:15 PM

"*THAT'S* WHY I couldn't press charges," Celia said as she applied iodine to the cut near my mouth. "Gerard always travels with that man, Basil. He's a sort of bodyguard and I knew he would be on board as well. If I had pressed charges against Gerard, Basil would have killed me. I'm sure of it."

"He's the man who followed me," I mumbled through my swollen cheek. The ship suddenly did a small dip and roll, causing Celia to press against my wound. "Ouch, watch it! Look, I don't understand why they waited so long to confront you or, rather, *us.* We've been out days now."

Celia slowly put the bandage roll back into the medicine cabinet. "I suppose Gerard was trying to figure out who you were and what he could get out of you before forcing you to turn me over to him."

I turned and looked at myself in the mirror. Considering the many blows I'd taken that day I was surprised that a sore shoulder, a slightly swollen jaw, and small cut on my right side were all I had to show. As I prodded my cheek, I found the wheels of my mind spinning. Celia's story seemed to keep evolving. She hadn't mentioned this Basil until he showed up. Yet then she said she had known immediately that he would be on board with Remy. But why was the bodyguard in first class and his boss in steerage? And why was she so intent on getting me out of the way? If the Frenchman was as violent as she claimed, surely she'd want the benefit of my protection—limited as today had proven it to be. She wasn't telling me everything, and contrary to her earlier plea, I now found myself trusting her less and less.

"And Remy—what does he want with you?" I asked.

Celia looked at me with confusion. "He wants me back—back with him."

"Why?"

She sat down on the edge of the bathtub. "I don't know how to answer that. He has a sort of obsession with me. It's not love—it's something else. He seems to enjoy controlling me, keeping me under this thumb."

I gave her a skeptical look.

"So this maniacal Frenchman races after you across England, books passage on a ship to America, and risks arrest—solely because of your great and undeniable beauty?" I asked with deliberate sarcasm.

Celia gave me a half indignant, half hurt look. "Never mind, Nigel. I can't begin to make you understand."

She got up and left the bathroom.

"There must be more," I insisted as I followed her into our stateroom. "For all I know, this is part of a scheme you have with this Remy character: dupe the English fool into booking passage, then frame him for some crime or other and make off with the money. Perhaps there is an even bigger game aboard the *Titanic* than you've shared."

Celia sighed loudly. She didn't even attempt a retort.

"We have a fifty-fifty agreement on all spoils, my love," I reminded her as I stretched out on my couch. "Whatever is afoot, I am *not* leaving. I am *not* taking another room, and I am *not* pretending to be separated from my dear wife. For richer or poorer, good times and bad, our marriage is going to endure for the extent of this voyage. In fact, I'm not letting you out of my sight."

"Now you sound just like him," she scoffed.

"I may sound like this villain, but don't worry," I said. "I won't give you a matching set of scars on the other side of your back."

Celia whipped around and gave me a look of enraged loathing.

"Get out," she fumed with an almost crazed intensity. "If you don't leave this instant, Nigel, I will go to Davies and confess everything. I told you I no longer care about the money, and I'm more than willing to prove it. *Get out!*"

She was trembling with anger as she picked up a heavy-looking gilded hand mirror. Recalling her excellent throwing arm—not to mention a day already filled with physical blows—I decided it probably best to make an exit.

I got up and went to the door. As I opened it, I hesitated.

"Look, Celia, that last comment was a bit rough. I'm sor—"

The mirror streaked across the room like a lightning bolt—and made blindingly painful contact with the non-injured left side of my mouth.

As it turned out, *I* was the one who would have book-ended scars.

CHAPTER 20

Nigel Bowen
Atlantic Ocean
Friday, April 12, 1912, 9:30 PM

OF COURSE THE only place to nurse my many injuries was the bar in the smoking room. It was noisy and crowded and smoke-filled and just what I needed. I had a few shots of whiskey and bought a round for a couple of Scots headed to a golfing holiday in the States. We laughed and drank, and they told me risqué jokes that were impossible to understand through their thick brogues. Old habits die hard, and I was just about to suggest a game of cards, when I looked up into the bar mirror and saw someone standing behind me across the smoking room: Basil.

Catching my eye, he lifted a stein of beer. I whipped around, only to be confronted with young Phil. "Bowen! I've been looking all over for you!"

I looked past him on both sides, but Basil was nowhere in sight.

"Did you see a large bald man when you came in?" I asked urgently.

Phil glanced around in puzzlement and shook his head.

"Can't say that I did. But what I can say is I'm awfully sorry about this morning and—"

I turned my head to look on the other side of the bar, and Phil's eyes bugged out at the sight of my swollen mouth and matching cuts.

"Good lord! Did *I* do all this damage?" he asked incredulously, as he took hold of my chin and pointed it toward the light.

"I don't think so, but then again I've rather lost track." I sighed as I shrugged him off and took a gulp of my whiskey. "You here to finish the job, then?"

He laughed and clapped a strong hand on my shoulder. "No, I wanted to apologize. I had a long walk with Miss Moore today—jolly nice girl, by the way! From what she said it sounds like I'm responsible for a great deal of talk. I caused you to blame your wife for a flirtation that was entirely one-sided. And I only made things worse by trying to come to her defense."

He nudged one of the Scots out of the way and signaled the bartender for a round. "Look here, I can't deny that I find your wife extremely charming and attractive, but she shouldn't pay the price for my foolish infatuation. I hope I haven't caused any true unpleasantness between you two."

I shrugged and said, "Mmm, 'unpleasantness' captures things pretty well, but don't worry. It has little to do with you."

I continued looking for Basil; the way he appeared and

disappeared unnerved me. But I was at least comforted by the fact that he'd been alone; it probably meant Remy was either still in detention or far below in steerage. Either way, if all Celia had told me was true, I was going to need to keep my wits—and defenses—at the ready. But *was* all she said true?

The bartender put down our drinks, and Phil eagerly picked his up. "Let's drink to Mrs. Bowen then!"

He downed his in one sure gulp. "I won't pry into what is going on, but I daresay it will soon pass. Why, a near-sighted ninety-year-old could see how much in love you two are."

I scowled and threw back the rest of my drink, and we talked for the next hour or so. Or rather, I talked and Phil proved a good sport by listening. I obviously couldn't go into the exact situation with Celia, but he patiently endured my general complaints about how unknowable women were and how I was vowing to stay clear of them from that point on. I signaled the bartender for another round, but Phil took me by the shoulders.

"I think you've again had more than your share," he said as he pulled me up from the stool. I protested a little, but as we walked I found myself swaying and bumping into people as he steered me toward the exit.

"A fierce swell tonight," I muttered. "Funny, I'm just now noticing it!"

Phil laughed to himself and we went out onto the deck. There was a cool breeze blowing across the wooden planks, but the ship was plowing forward through the sea smoothly, and it was only then that I realized I was stinking drunk. What's more, I was suddenly overcome with the urgent need to be sick. Phil guessed my condition and quickly maneuvered me down the deck to a rail that was flush against the side of the liner.

I leaned over and stared into the nearly black churning water. It was a strange sensation—like I was flying across the ocean—and even at this high level I felt a spray of water on my face. I wondered what it would be like to fall the great distance down into the sea. How hard would the water be when a body hit? How cold was that roiling water?

Eventually the sick feeling passed. I turned around and leaned my back against the rail and now looked up at the starry but moonless night. The decks of the *Titanic* glowed under their faint light, and I saw the very distinct figure of a large man up on the furthermost compass platform. He was leaning against the railing, looking down at me. Of course it was Basil, and though we couldn't make out each other's eyes, I held his stare for a long time.

The effect became dizzying and I suddenly felt almost hypnotized. My body went limp, and I started to roll backward over the rail. I was dimly aware of Phil shouting and grabbing me around the waist. For a moment I looked "up" to see the ocean directly above me.

Phil yanked me back over the side. "Watch it, chap! Look, it's awfully late and you're sure to waken Mrs. Bowen. You'd better bunk with me for the night."

I nodded at Phil's offer, and as we started back down the deck, I tried to avoid looking up at the compass platform. But my curiosity got the better of me. I glanced up and—again, exactly as expected—Basil was gone.

But in his place: a short, muscular man with curly hair.

CHAPTER 21

Celia Bowen
Atlantic Ocean
Saturday, April 13, 1912, 5:00 PM

I WAS TOO afraid to leave the cabin the entire day.

Nigel hadn't come back the previous night. The morning wore on and then it was afternoon and he still hadn't returned. I paced and paced as the ship rolled through a lengthy swell that evening. The circumstances that had looked so rosy just over twenty-four hours ago had turned utterly against me. I felt trapped on all sides and kept wishing there were some way to get off this boat even though it was in the middle of the Atlantic Ocean.

I started at a sudden knock. I hesitantly went over to the door and asked who it was. The reply came back "Steward, ma'am," and, indeed, a capped young man stood there. He presented me with a small card and, tipping his hat, walked away. I closed the door and opened the note, which read:

Dearest Celia,

Do join your new friend for late tea tomorrow at 4:30.

Beryl Sedgwick

So she needed another fistful of cash. I sighed in frustration, and just then another knock sounded. I pulled the door back open without thinking.

Gerard Remy stood there.

He was now dressed in gentlemen's garb—an impeccable suit and tie—and he was freshly shaved. I backed away in mute horror and stumbled as the ship again did a gradual side-to-side roll. Gerard gave me a strangely gentle smile and walked into the room. He closed the door behind him—and locked it.

"Good evening," he said in the heavily accented voice that had once made me swoon. "Such a strange relief to speak English again! I've been pretending not to understand a word to those officers since I saw you yesterday. Thank you, darling Molly, for suggesting it."

He took a seat on Nigel's couch and looked around the room. "Hmm, Basil's cabin has *two* windows. But still, this is much nicer than where I've been bunking in steerage."

He looked at me in a friendly manner that was so false it was chilling.

"Gerard...listen. I'm going to have a great deal of money after we dock," I said as calmly as possible. "We've—Mr. Bowen and I—we've had a bit of luck. But it all hangs on it looking as though we are happily mar—"

"You are wondering why Basil booked a room on the *Titanic,* are you not?" he asked, ignoring me. "I had such an odd feeling that our scheme—you recall our great scheme, darling? I felt something might go wrong. So I made a number of—what is the term—*contingencies,* yes? I suspected your dedication to our plan was weak so I found another girl, a pretty and willing wench named Liselle, just in case you disappointed me. As, of course, you did."

He didn't glare or sound angry—he just sat as calmly as if we were enjoying a cup of tea together. "Alas, it turned out Miss Liselle was a bit *too* taken with the plot. I discovered she had designs to use it herself with another partner! Can you imagine? Meanwhile, I booked passage for you and I on the *Olympic* and—again—just in case—Basil booked the *Titanic.* Fortunate, yes?"

My mind was reeling. If there had been a larger window, I might well have jumped out of it. I took a seat next to him and looked into his eyes.

"Gerard, I can't do it. That's why I left you. I just *can't* do it. I'll give you whatever I have—but I can't go through with anything involving a child. I beg you!" I pleaded.

"Pickpocketing drunk rich men is one thing, but *kidnapping* is—"

He stood up sharply. "I dislike that word. We are simply *borrowing* the child of a rich couple until they realize that twenty-five-thousand dollars isn't much to spare their tot from being tossed into the sea. And you *are* going to help, dear *Mrs. Bowen*."

I stood up from the couch. "Gerard, please. Nigel—Mr. Bowen—has *nothing* to do with any of this. Please leave him out of it."

He looked at me silently for a long, unnerving moment. Then, with a cold smile, he reached out and took my hands. "You are quite taken with this man, and on such short acquaintance. I wonder...how well do you really know him?"

He continued staring at me. "You must realize that Basil was trailing you all last week, my dear. He tells me your last evening in Southampton as a fetching redhead was quite eventful: card games, brawls, escapes. But there was more adventure for Mr. Bowen once you parted ways that night. You see, Basil followed Mr. Bowen and witnessed a rendezvous with yet another young lady—one he took to his hotel. But the encounter did not end quite so well for her. It seems a heated argument led to one thing and then, well, *quite* another..."

"What are you talking about?" I asked, though I instantly knew; asking was just a way of delaying the news.

"Surely you heard about the notorious 'Southampton Strangler'?"

"That's—that's ridiculous!" I stuttered angrily. I tried to pull away, but he narrowed his eyes and held my hands more forcefully.

"I see you've suspected all along," he said with a smirk.

I felt I could barely breathe. It didn't seem possible. I knew Nigel was a thief and a cheat, but I couldn't believe he was capable of being a killer. Then again, he *was* acting strangely nervous the morning we left. And he was awfully insistent about using the Bjornstroms' name *before* we sailed, though he didn't seem to give it a second thought once we pulled out of the dock.

Still, though it was true I did not know Nigel well, I *did* know Gerard Remy.

"You're lying," I said in a strangled whisper.

"Poor Molly." He sighed with fake sympathy. "Now she doesn't know whom she should trust—that nasty Mr. Remy or the mysterious Mr. Bowen. But don't fret. You and your *husband* can continue to keep secrets from each other. Mr. Bowen need not be involved or know anything of our plot—if you help us. But if you do not, be assured that I will reveal his identity to the ship's officers—if Basil doesn't kill him first. Basil is rather a hothead, you know. At any rate, the choice is yours, *ma belle*."

I pulled my hands from his, but he held them; squeezed

them. I looked up and it was then I saw in his eyes the first honest expression he'd displayed: the cruelty I knew so well. He began crushing my hands until I was in agonizing pain and I fell to the floor. Just then, there was yet another knock on the door. He released me and, using his foot, shoved me toward the door.

Shaking with pain, anger, and humiliation, I got up and unlocked it.

It was Nigel.

"All right, my girl, I've had all day to think, and I've come to make up," he said sheepishly. "Also, I *must* change my clothes. Young Phil's not my size, and I'm beginning to smell like I've been shoveling coal in the engine ro—"

Before I could stop him, he walked past me into the room. Gerard was again sitting coolly on the couch. Nigel gaped at him for a moment, then whipped around to look at me with a startled and confused—and furious—glare.

"So it *has* been you and him all along!" he spat out.

I involuntarily started toward Nigel, but just then the great ship made yet another rocking motion. The movement gave me a moment to pause and think. Whoever or whatever Nigel was, I had recruited him in a plan to rob wealthy passengers, nothing more. It was my obligation to shield him from Gerard.

Gathering every bit of willpower I had, I went past Nigel to the couch. I lowered myself to the floor at Gerard's feet and took his hand. Trembling inside, I looked up to Nigel.

"Yes, it's been him all along, darling," I said as flippantly as I could. "Maybe you can *finally* understand why your constant advances were so tiresome to me."

I had to do it—I had to be brutal. And it worked. Nigel paled with hurt and fury.

"I don't know what game this is or what you two are after," he fumed savagely. "But I swear this: I will do *everything* in my power to ensure that it ends in disaster."

With a bitter parting look, he slammed the door on us.

The *Titanic* dipped again, righted itself, and sailed on.

CHAPTER 22

Celia Bowen

Atlantic Ocean

Sunday, April 14, 1912, 6:00 PM

THOUGH THE SEA had calmed, I still walked uneasily down the first class promenade—my legs wobbled as though we were sailing through a monsoon. Up ahead I saw Herbert and Violet Vogel and their son, Arthur. They were with Emily Moore, as I knew they would be. Earlier that day I had learned from the girl that she would be looking after young Arthur while the Vogels dined. The brightly dressed little boy jumped around excitedly—eager to start whatever fun and games Emily had promised him.

The weather had taken a chilly turn and everyone was bundled up. Not fifteen feet beyond the small group, I saw Basil half hidden behind a bulkhead, watching them. He looked up and gave me a curt nod. Despite the cold, I felt a hot flash of shame course through my body.

I slowed my approach—the last thing I wanted was interaction with Arthur's parents. But Mrs. Vogel turned and, seeing me, gave a small, pitying smile. Leaving the others, she approached me.

"We're so disappointed you won't be joining our little dinner, Mrs. Bowen," the dark-haired, petite woman said sadly. "But—well, your husband has explained the situation."

I had no idea what she was talking about, and she must have read my confused silence as offense.

"I certainly don't mean to pry," she said hastily. "But I truly hope you two can work things out. Mr. Bowen has such kindness in his heart."

She gave my arm a friendly pat and then turned back to her group. Just then Nigel joined them and I realized he must have made some dinner arrangement for us. Catching sight of me in the corner of his eye, he scowled darkly and led the Vogels away.

Emily grasped Arthur's hand and the two began a little skip up the promenade. I hesitated, then glanced at Basil, who frowned and jerked his head in their direction. I forced myself to follow.

For a time, Emily and Arthur went up and down several decks and appeared to be playing some kind of chase game, but the older girl always kept a watchful eye on her charge. Basil remained just a few feet behind, silently goading me on. At one point they met up with Mr. Colley. He delayed them for quite some time—a flirtation had clearly sprung up between he and Miss Moore. While they were talking I was able to hide behind a group of walkers and move unseen past them. Positioning myself in a corner up ahead, I looked back and saw Arthur was insisting that they continue playing. Phil reluctantly moved on—with several glances back at Miss Moore's retreating figure.

I turned so that I was facing three-quarters towards the sea. Without any pretending, my shoulders started to heave and a series of sobs broke out of me.

As I had planned—and feared—I suddenly heard: *"Mrs. Bowen!"*

I slowly turned and Emily was standing next to me.

"You poor *dear!* Standing out here shivering and sobbing—and all because of that awful man!" She fumed while still glancing toward Arthur who was now scrambling over a nearby deck chair.

Emily took hold of my shoulders and gave me a stern woman-to-woman look. "I'm only telling you this because I have heard the marriage is over: Mr. Bowen tried to make love to me our second day out! You are *well* rid of him!"

"Yes—yes…That's what everyone says," I said, weeping and for a moment unable to get any further words out. Basil walked by and gave me a threatening glare over Emily's shoulder. She seemed about to turn away so I burst into fresh tears. "But—but *still*—I can't help but…"

I fell into a kind of faint and Emily blindly reached out to stop my fall. She led me to an empty deck chair and helped me into it. Behind her I caught a lightning-quick glimpse of Basil grasping Arthur's hand. I closed my eyes and an unplanned and uncontrollable wail poured out.

Emily looked at me with true alarm. "We must get you to the ship's doctor at once! Let me just collect Arthur and we'll—"

She looked around from one side to another.

"Arthur! *Arthur!*" she called out in annoyance. "He was right over there just seconds ago. Oh, dear. *ARTHUR!*"

I couldn't go through with it. I immediately leapt up and ran in the direction Basil had moved. Surely I could still stop this from happening. "This way!" I cried to Emily.

Emily paused, confused and worried. "Are you sure? Did you see him?"

"No—I…" I stumbled. "Well, why don't I go this way and you go the other? One of us is sure to find him!"

Emily instantly agreed and we parted. I hurriedly dodged my way through the crowds looking for any sign of Arthur or Basil.

After moving up and down endless corridors and decks in a desperate and increasingly pointless search, I eventually met up with the now truly alarmed Emily on the Bridge Deck. There was nothing to do but go to the Vogels' room in the hope—futile, I knew—that the boy had been returned there. In our panic we had forgotten that they were on their way to dinner, so after checking the dining saloon, we went to the Verandah Café and Café Parisien before finally locating them in the À la Carte Restaurant. I noticed that Nigel wasn't with the party. Emily ran to them, just as a steward handed Mr. Vogel a piece of paper, which he read. He immediately turned ashen and started shaking.

I couldn't go over there and pretend to that terrified and frantic couple that I didn't know what was happening. After wavering a moment, I decisively turned and ran down the passage.

The plan was for me to return to my room where Gerard was waiting; I was to provide his alibi by calling in a steward who would see us together. Though I was deliberately kept in the dark about the details, I had overheard Gerard and Basil mention the mail storage room on one of the lowest decks as a possible ransom drop-off location. It was apparently a remote spot, and I gambled that Basil might be holding the boy somewhere nearby.

Making my way down was difficult; I had but a vague idea of the layout of the ship beyond first class. I only knew that the post office was toward the front on G Deck, directly below the squash court and barely above the water line. The mail sorting room was underneath the post office and would surely be deserted at this late hour. Twice I had to turn back when kindly stewards pointed me back toward my "appropriate" area.

Finally, after many dead ends, I came upon the darkened

mail storage hold. It was terribly quiet, and my leather heels echoed loudly in the narrow passage. No one seemed to be about, and the sorting room door and the other nearby doors were all locked. As I turned to see if there was a back way into the hold, I was suddenly slammed against the wall.

My head hit the surface with a force that stunned me. I slid helplessly to the floor in a sort of whiplashed daze and dimly registered Gerard's furious face. Though in a stupor, I still found myself wondering how he'd found me. Then I realized he'd known all along that I couldn't go through with the plot and had obviously followed me. I must have momentarily blacked out, for the next thing I was aware of was being shoved into a darkened hold. I landed in a heap, my head pounding and the wind knocked out of me.

A small voice piped up out of the near darkness.

"Did you bring my dog, Ladybelle? That ugly man promised to take me to her, but I don't see her anywhere…"

CHAPTER 23

Nigel Bowen
Atlantic Ocean
Sunday, April 14, 1912, 11:30 PM

I WAS BEGINNING to wonder if it might not make sense to transfer my belongings out of Phil's room and into the smoking room; I was certainly spending enough time there lately. I was supposed to have dinner with the Vogels, and had been on my way to the restaurant with them, but since Celia had revealed her true self, I didn't very much feel like being around other people. I begged their forgiveness, claiming that I didn't feel well, and after promising Mrs. Vogel that I would go see the doctor right away, I went back to Phil's suite, where the events of the past five days finally caught up with me. I slept for several hours. When I woke up I had no other place to go, so I entered the smoking room for a drink. The first person I saw was Randolph Davies.

I'd managed to avoid him since the scene with Emily at the lower deck staircase. Now he was sitting alone at the bar and studying a telegram. After a moment, he placed it inside his coat pocket and then grimaced painfully, as though he'd poked a wound. Looking up, he gave me a strange half smile. I decided to meet matters head-on.

"Good evening, Mr. Davies," I said formally. "No doubt you've heard that I've utterly failed in my attempts at sobriety—not to mention physical restraint—and that my marriage is at an end. On a positive note, I've saved you a great deal of money."

To my surprise he gave a bitter chuckle—a slightly drunken one.

"My boy, I hope you live to be as old as I," he said, sounding tired. "You'll learn that money ultimately matters very little. I don't know why you pretend to be a swine and I no longer care. But take my advice: Find your wife, kiss her with all the longing you so obviously feel, and to hell with all the rest of it."

At that, he pushed himself up from the bar and staggered toward the door. My astonishment lasted only seconds as Mr. Davies's exit coincided with the entrance of Herbert Vogel and a stricken-looking Emily Moore. Women were a rare sight in the smoking room so I immediately knew something was amiss.

"Mr. Bowen, we've been looking all over for you! I beg you to help us!" Vogel said desperately. His hands were shaking as he gave me a note. In deliberately crude block letters it read:

IF YOU WISH TO SEE MASTER ARTHUR AGAIN, DROP
OFF $25,000 CASH IN A SMALL SUITCASE OUTSIDE THE
MARCONI OFFICE AT 1:00 AM. IF YOU FAIL OR IF YOU
ALERT ANY AUTHORITIES, ARTHUR WILL BE TOSSED OVER
THE RAIL.

Of course my immediate thought was Remy and Celia. So this was it, the real reason they had boarded the ship. Despite my hatred of Remy and the disgust I felt at Celia for being involved in such a low operation, I had to acknowledge that theirs was a first-rate plan. They had all the cards. The child could be anywhere on the massive ship and could be disposed of in seconds if the need arose.

I shoved the note into my pocket and steered Vogel and Emily to the darkened side of the room. "I can't go into how I know this, but you must trust what I tell you. The man who took Arthur is a Frenchman named Gerard Remy. He is being helped by—by..." I hesitated long enough for the two to look at me questioningly. "By a tall, bald Englishman named Basil. We have to search the ship from top to bottom."

"Come now, Mr. Bowen! Surely we must alert the officers," Emily said to me dismissively; she clearly still held a grudge. "How on earth can the three of us cover the *entire* ship?"

"If we go to an officer, I assure you these men will carry

out their threat," I said heatedly. She was, of course, right that we stood no chance of searching the whole of the *Titanic*. I looked around in frustration and spotted Phil coming through the entrance. His face lit up at the sight of Emily but just as quickly fell when he saw our grave expressions. After flagging him over, I quickly filled the young man in on the extraordinary developments. As he listened with amazement, Vogel spoke up.

"We will *never* find these kidnappers!" Vogel insisted, sick with worry. "And I *have* the money. Violet's aunt gave it to us in London. She distrusts banks and insisted we take a large amount of cash to use for Arthur's education."

I wondered how Remy could possibly have known that, but I didn't have time to dwell on it.

"You'll pay only as a last resort. The money is the only leveraging power you have," I warned. "For now, we search. Phil, you, and Miss Moore take first class. It's unlikely they would hold Arthur so near his parents, but then again, they might just be counting on our thinking that. Vogel, you search the second class quarters. I'll take steerage. If you see either of these men, do *nothing* except follow them. We'll meet back here in thirty minutes."

I hurriedly gave them more detailed physical descriptions of Remy and Basil. We then checked our watches and started out. But as I held open the door for Emily, something curious happened. A pronounced trembling suddenly ran through the ship. It started low and increased quickly in strength. The four of us looked at one another in puzzlement, and I had the absurd idea that the great liner had abruptly gone aground and run across a billion marbles.

As we stepped into the bitter night cold, I saw a man leaning over the deck rail excitedly pointing toward the front of the ship.

"We hit an iceberg—there it is!"

CHAPTER 24

Nigel Bowen
Atlantic Ocean
Sunday, April 14, 1912, 11:45 PM

I PEERED INTO the night and saw a large, dark shape. There was no moon, but by the dim light of the stars I was able to make out the floating mountain of ice.

"We went right up against it!" the man was yelling. "Ice fell on the decks below!"

"An *iceberg?*" Emily said, squinting out at the sea. "But that's ridiculous!"

"Actually, we've been sailing through fields of ice since this afternoon," Philip observed with a touch of concern in his voice. He took Emily's hand. "Perhaps you should go to your father, Miss Moore."

"Absolutely *not!*" she protested. "It's *completely* my fault that Arthur was taken, and I won't rest until he is found!"

Curious passengers began spilling out onto the deck to see what the commotion was about, and nearly all seemed taken aback by the fierce cold.

"Maybe we can use this to our advantage if we act

quickly," I said. "Remy and Basil are bound to come out to see what is happening. Everyone search the outside decks of your assigned area!"

But just as we began to separate, something even more curious—and alarming—occurred.

The *Titanic* came to a complete stop.

Everyone milling about on the decks looked around in confusion. Excited and puzzled questions were met by shrugs and even tipsy laughter. But suddenly a deafening roar drowned the voices out. We all looked up to see the four massive funnels releasing great billowing clouds of steam into the still night air.

I didn't take time to observe more. I hurried to the nearest crew ladder, as I guessed it would be the fastest way to get to the lower decks. As I dodged through the gathering crowds on the Bridge Deck, where most of the first class cabins were located, I nearly toppled a harried-looking woman wearing a heavy fur coat over a pink nightgown—Mrs. Sedgwick.

"Mr. Bowen!" she cried. "What in heaven's name is this ruckus about? Why have we stopped?"

"There's talk of an iceberg, Mrs. Sedgwick," I said hurriedly as I tried to pass her. "It seems we might have brushed up against one."

The older woman reached out and grabbed my coat. "What nonsense! I won't *stand* for any kind of delay to our schedule. Just as I will not stand for your wife neglecting her obligation to me!"

I stopped and turned to her. "What are you talking about?"

She gave a snide laugh.

"Just tell *Mrs. Bowen*," she said with sarcastic emphasis, "that I expect her the very *first* thing in the morning. Tell her it regards our mutual friend 'Molly.'"

At that, Mrs. Sedgwick turned and vanished into the crowd of excited nannies and ladies' maids cluttering the passage. I didn't have time to try to sort out her meaning and so, irritated and perplexed, I pushed my way through the crowd and hurried down another deck.

As I entered a second-class cabin area, I saw a chubby steward addressing a small crowd of passengers in the hallway. Most were clad in robes and bedclothes; their looks ranged from sleepy to worried to irritated.

"There's absolutely *nothing* to be alarmed about, ladies and gents. Standard ship maintenance is all," he was saying, sounding quite unconcerned and cheerful, perhaps even enjoying his moment of commanding the troops. "Please go back to your cabins. And a very good night to you all!"

As he smiled broadly, another steward hastily made his way over and whispered something to him. I thought the hefty steward paled a little.

"Er…then again, it seems the captain is being extra cautious," he blustered to the crowd. "This is purely routine, mind you, but all passengers are being asked, well, to put on the lifebelts that can found in all cabins—"

The assembled either gasped in fear or groaned at the inconvenience.

As I continued on my way toward steerage, I wondered if there was any real possibility of the ship being in danger. I looked up to see two junior officers rushing by.

"—and *he* said the watertight doors were all *closed*," one whispered urgently.

"Yes, but the tear extends past more than one compartment and—"

Glancing over, the officer saw my startled expression. He grabbed his companion's arm and hurried him farther along out of my hearing.

A tear in the *Titanic*'s hull? At our first dinner the officer had told us that the steel plates were almost two inches thick—how was a tear even conceivable? Was the ship to be stranded in the middle of the ocean? My mind raced over the possibilities. Surely something like this would cause Remy to release the child, I reasoned. Then again, I doubted there could be any reasoning with that fiend—*or* with Celia.

Continuing on my way down into the bowels of the ship, I couldn't help but reflect that Celia's true identity had been discovered by Mrs. Sedgwick...and the older woman was quite obviously blackmailing Celia, shocking as the act was for a woman of her social rank. How long had the extortion been going on? I recalled the older woman's pointed questions to Celia our first night out. Did she know immediately? Why hadn't Celia told me? How much was the old bitch demanding?

I angrily shook my head free of these thoughts. None of this was my concern. Celia had betrayed me and broken our agreement; I would be glad to see her exposed. Sedgwick surely knew that Celia's freedom was at stake and was bound to demand a hefty price to keep quiet, an amount Celia couldn't possibly meet unless—unless—

Unless she helped Remy in his kidnapping plot.

I stumbled against the passage wall in the middle of F Deck. For a moment I thought it was because my mind was reeling from thoughts of Celia and her perhaps unwitting involvement in the despicable kidnapping plot. But I suddenly realized that my balance had been thrown because the passage had taken on a noticeable decline toward the front of the ship—and was listing heavily to the starboard side.

The steepness of the angle was such that it could mean only one astonishing thing.

The *Titanic* was sinking.

CHAPTER 25

Celia Bowen
Atlantic Ocean
Monday, April 15, 1912, 1:00 AM

"LET US OUT—*let us out*—*LET US OUT!"*

We both paused to listen for a moment, then Arthur again started kicking the door. He struck at it repeatedly, and the whole time he kept glancing up at me, amazed that I was letting him get away with such blatant misbehavior. I didn't understand how the noise we were making couldn't be heard on the outside. Earlier there had seemed to be some kind of commotion going on farther down the passage. I guessed it had something to do with the curious rumbling we had heard and the fact that the ship had inexplicably stopped. But since then, all had been silent.

Luckily, Arthur seemed to find the situation a great adventure and had pointed out several times that this was the latest he'd ever stayed up. I tried to pretend that we had been accidentally locked in the postal hold, that this was a game of hide-and-seek and that the other players had simply gotten lost while looking for us. But after thirty minutes or so, Arthur started asking for his mother. I then changed the game to Who Can Yell the Loudest? but with no success at attracting attention from the outside.

I knew Gerard had demanded that the Vogels drop off the money at 1:00 a.m., so I told myself that he would be releasing us soon after. Even his vile presence would be welcome after such a long time in the dark, stuffy mail cargo hold. There seemed to be only one electric ceiling light, and without windows it was difficult to see beyond the shadowy stacks of mailbags that seemed to go on forever, one piled on top of another. I was about to explore again to see if there was something I could use to pound on the door when it suddenly clicked open.

Though the hulking figure standing there was backlit by the outside passage light, I knew immediately that it was Basil. He stepped into the room and locked the door behind him.

"My dog *isn't* in here," Arthur said angrily to him. "You're a big fat *liar!*"

"Here now, that's no way to talk to your old pal, is it, sonny?" Basil said in a strained attempt at sounding friendly. He worked his mouth into something resembling a smile, but the look he shot my way was pure contempt. "If anyone here is a liar, it's the *lady*. She's gone and broken her promises to her friends. That's not right, is it, sonny?"

Arthur looked back and forth at us in bewilderment,

clearly not used to an adult asking him to weigh in on the actions of another. I stepped forward.

"Please, Bas—"

"Don't use my name in front of him, you bloody *fool!*" he hissed at me. He then tried again to assume a smile for Arthur's benefit. He took the boy's shoulder and continued on in a paternal voice. "See, she's not been playing by the rules. And bad things can happen to such ladies. Why, just look at what happened to my dear friend…Miss Liselle."

Basil pointedly looked at me and I had to stifle a gasp. In a flash I realized what should have been plainly obvious to me all along: Basil had murdered this young woman, Liselle, after she double-crossed Remy—and he'd framed Nigel in the process. The police were after Nigel and he knew it—why hadn't he told me? We had kept so much from each other—and all it had achieved was to increase the danger of our circumstances.

I backed away from Basil, though there were only a few feet of space I could move in. The fact that he had revealed this information left no doubt as to his intentions for me. But I was desperate to save the child. I quickly scanned the room again—if only there was something I could use as a weapon!

Then it dawned on me.

I just needed to get Arthur away from Basil's side. I slowly took a step toward the large man.

"But we *like* changing rules, don't we, Arthur?" I asked with a wry smile, never taking my eyes off of Basil's. "It makes games so much more fun."

I continued toward Basil until I was directly in front of him, my chest slightly pressed against his. "It makes things more...*thrilling*."

Basil stared at me with a mix of confusion, fury, and something else. And that something else was just what I was hoping for. I had always suspected that despite his brutal demeanor, Basil was deeply conflicted about women, perhaps even a little afraid of them.

"Let's play a *new* game of hide-and-seek, Arthur," I said with a quick glance down at the boy. "You go hide...but this time the gentleman and I will turn out the light and will have to look for you *in the dark!*"

I reached up and lightly drew my finger across Basil's lips. I lowered my voice to a whisper. "It could take a very long time...in total darkness."

Basil's whole body seemed to tremble and small beads of sweat broke out on his forehead. He narrowed his eyes menacingly at me, but an involuntary gulp gave away his discomfort. I continued trailing my fingertips over his lips, then slowly drew them across his cheek to his ear. I caressed his lobe softly. Basil glanced down at Arthur, then at the electric light switch on the wall. He hesitated, then slowly reached his arm out toward the switch. I saw that his hand was shaking slightly. He hesitated again and that's when I screamed, *"Run, Arthur!"*

The child darted forward and I quickly reached up behind Basil's head for one of the mailbags that were stacked directly above him. Grasping the heavy canvas tote, I yanked it down with all my might. The extraordinary weight of the bag fell directly on Basil's right shoulder, knocking him sideways to the ground. He barked out in rage but I swiftly kicked him in the midsection—again and then again. I was astonished at my own savagery. Basil doubled over in pain but still swung his arms out at my legs. He had apparently been holding the keys the entire time as they flew across the room when he thrashed about.

"Get the keys, Arthur!" I cried.

But the poor little boy just stood there, wide-eyed and stupefied. I flung myself forward and pulled down two more mailbags. They landed heavily on Basil, pinning him to the ground, though I knew it would only be for a moment. I wildly looked about for the keys and saw them glinting just under a wheeled mail bin. I dove at them and took hold of Arthur.

As I pulled him to the door, Basil shot a hand out and grabbed my ankle. I kicked blindly at him while fumbling with the keys. I couldn't get the first one in the slot, so I grappled with the second. It slid into the lock as if pulled by a magnet.

I tugged the door open and pushed Arthur out into the passage. Basil retained his grip on my ankle even as I shut the door on his wrist. The pain eventually made him release my leg, but he then grasped the edge of the door, refusing to let it close even as I pressed so hard that his fingers were surely smashed.

Finally he had to give up and pulled in his wounded paw. I slammed the door and locked it. After a moment's hesitation, I left the key in the lock. I then pulled Arthur up into my arms and started running down the passageway.

I was so panicked, I barely even noticed that— inexplicably—I seemed to be running downhill.

CHAPTER 26

Celia Bowen
Atlantic Ocean
Monday, April 15, 1912, 1:15 AM

I HAD NO real idea where I was headed—I wanted only to get as far from Basil as possible. At the end of the corridor I nearly collided with a group of uniformed men who were barreling toward the mail compartment.

"Please! You must help me," I cried out. The men wore expressions of intense concern and barely glanced at me as they rushed by.

"Sorry, no time, miss," the youngest one said while the others were speaking over each other.

"—but it will be impossible to get *all* the mail bags on deck!" one of them breathlessly shouted after the two in front. The oldest man, who I took to be some sort of senior official, barked back, "We'll get the Priority Mail—the rest will have to be abandoned!"

What on earth was going on? They were headed directly to the mail hold so I knew Basil would be released in seconds. Grabbing Arthur, I quickly guided us down an empty corridor and then into another that turned out to be a dead end. Doubling back and taking the next short corridor, we suddenly came into a larger hallway that was overflowing with people.

They were all steerage passengers, and by their unusual dress and the variety of accents I heard, I guessed most to be foreign. Many were simply standing in the passage looking confused or even bored, though two young men were laughing and tossing a lifebelt back and forth. But just as many men and women were clutching their children and—bizarrely—their luggage. They were moving uncertainly up the passage in the opposite direction Arthur and I were headed. The excitement in the air made me wonder if word had spread about the kidnapping and perhaps a general alert had gone out to the other parents aboard.

I hesitated for a moment, unsure if I should continue on alone toward the front of the ship or fall in with the crowd and risk running directly into Basil. Suddenly, a gray-haired middle-aged woman stopped in front of me and shook my arm.

"*Bitte,* take my child *up!*" she cried in a heavy German accent. I stared at her, perplexed, as she had no child. She shook her head in frustration and pointed at Arthur. "Take my child *up! Bitte!*"

I suddenly realized she was using the wrong pronoun and had meant to say "*your* child."

"Why?" I asked. "What is happening?"

"The ship is *down!*" she said urgently, while pointing her finger at the floor. Suddenly an older man approached. He took her elbow and tried to pull her away. They argued fiercely in German until the woman finally gave in and motioned frantically for me to join them in going up the passage.

I looked out over the crowd—and there was Basil, pushing and shoving his way directly toward us.

"I'm tired," Arthur said, on the verge of tears. "I want my mother *now*."

"She's this way, Arthur!"

I pulled the whimpering boy in the opposite direction of Basil and we darted down a long, eerily deserted side passage. We ran for what seemed like half the ship's length. Then I paused as I noticed that in addition to the downhill slant of the corridor there was now a pronounced shift to the right. I scarcely had time to consider what it all meant when my foot suddenly splashed through water.

I looked down and saw that there was a shallow pool at our feet—and I quickly felt that it was ice cold. With horror, I realized it was seawater.

Was it *possible?* Surely the ship wasn't in serious danger, I told myself. Everyone knew the *Titanic* had been declared unsinkable.

But the water was rising at an alarming rate; it almost immediately went past our ankles to our shins.

"Why is there water, miss?" Arthur asked with worried curiosity.

"A—a pipe," I stuttered, trying for calm. "A pipe must have broken. We'll go to your mother the other way."

We turned around but just as we did, I heard a bursting sound from behind and something began roaring up the passage. I tried to push Arthur to run but a hill of water instantly engulfed us and knocked us both face forward. We gasped at the cold, and I struggled to stand so I could pull the boy up. But before I could, someone reached out and grabbed Arthur by the neck of his jacket—Basil.

He lifted the panicked child and went to use his other hand to strike me—but that one was dripping blood and several fingers hung at strange angles. Instead, he spat at me and pulled Arthur away.

The lights in the hallway started to flicker and it seemed that the entire area would be flooded in minutes. I lunged wildly at Basil and, reaching out in desperation, I seized his broken hand. He yelped at the mere touch, and though it was agony for me to do it, I squeezed his hand hard, as cruelly as Gerard had crushed mine.

"*Bloody bitch!*" Basil cursed. In his pain, he toppled over into the water and inadvertently released the child.

I shoved Arthur forward into what had become a strong current. Basil furiously splashed about behind us, trying to get up using his one good hand. With the water already almost at my waist, I took hold of a side rail and pulled Arthur and I to an intersecting passage. Doing a sort of running swim, we made it across the corridor just as a new influx of water poured in from the other direction. The two raging streams slapped together, creating a shifting swirl of currents. I turned to see Basil caught up in it; despite his great strength, he was knocked backward. He again struggled to get up but the water was now surging from seemingly every direction, creating a gurgling whirlpool directly around him. Suddenly—and with startling quickness—the vortex sucked him under.

He never came up.

I moved Arthur to my shoulders, and as he clasped his arms around my neck, I swam toward the staircase at the end of the passage.

CHAPTER 27

Celia Bowen
Atlantic Ocean
Monday, April 15, 1912, 1:30 AM

DESPITE THE LOUD rush of the water I could hear panicked voices and much running and stomping on the passage above us. I tried to scream, but my lungs were seized up from the cold. As I painfully pulled and swam toward the staircase, Arthur kicked his little legs in an effort to help. The water jostled about suddenly and the movement lifted us up—just enough so that I was able to cling to the staircase rail. I slowly pulled us forward until my feet finally touched on the stairs beneath the water.

I climbed up as through quicksand, almost weeping with relief and gratitude when I finally stepped out of the water and onto the passage. All sorts of people—stewards, officers, cooks, mothers and their children—were rushing by. Some were terrified and crying, others seemed strangely excited. Though all about us was chaos, I was dimly aware of romantic music being played by a far-off orchestra.

I swung the thoroughly soaked Arthur forward off my shoulders—directly into Gerard's waiting arms.

He'd appeared out of nowhere.

Gerard wrapped a blanket around Arthur almost tenderly. Any one of the alarmed passengers and crew rushing past might have thought he was the boy's concerned father.

"What's happening?" I cried. "Is the ship really sinking?"

He adjusted the blanket around the freezing child on his hip and gently patted his back. Arthur stared at him with blank confusion.

"Atrocious timing, isn't it? But as I told you, I had bad feelings about this scheme from the beginning." Remy sighed. "Yes, it appears that the *Titanic is* sinking. And it seems the only way I can board a lifeboat is if I accompany a child. So I'm afraid as the ship goes down, *mon belle,* you go with it."

He kicked out his foot. It landed in the middle of my stomach, sending me reeling backward. I plunged again into the freezing water—the shock of Gerard's action compounded by the shock of icy-cold water.

I flailed about wildly and tried to right myself in order to swim, but the current dragged me away from the stairs back down the corridor. Because of the tilt of the ship, the farther down the passage I was carried, the higher the water was to the ceiling. I wasn't even trying to swim at this point—I was just grasping about in the dark water, trying desperately to cling to anything I could grab.

The back of my wrist slammed against a hard metal surface. I reached out with my other hand and took hold of what I quickly realized was the rung of a ladder up to the next deck. My strength was all but gone; still, I clung with what little I had left.

Looking up through the opening in the deck floor, I could see people rushing about, but all I could hear was the roiling water, now rising faster than ever. There was no way I could pull myself out of the portal. I let out one final scream—a choking inhuman sound that I knew no one could hear over the turmoil.

I felt all the fight slip out of me. I closed my eyes in exhaustion and surrender. As I let go of the rung, a hand suddenly plunged down and roughly took hold of my forearm. In spite of the numbness coursing through my body, a shot of pain ripped down my arm from where the hand gripped me with astonishing strength. For a moment I tried to fight it—by now I *wanted* to let go.

But my eyes flew open and through my tears and the stinging salt water I saw a face looking down at me.

It was Nigel Bowen.

CHAPTER 28

Celia Bowen
Atlantic Ocean
Monday, April 15, 1912, 1:55 AM

"HOW...HOW..." I tried to speak but was overwhelmed by cold and fatigue. Nigel seemed to be dragging me up several decks, one after another, but I was completely disoriented as to where we were. I just knew that the tilt of the passage was getting steeper and steeper.

"How did I find you?" Nigel asked as he pulled me along. "I heard your scream. I'd only heard it once before—but I knew I'd never forget it."

"Nigel...I have so much to tell you," I gasped. "That girl who was murdered—Gerard and Basil framed you!"

I could feel the shock run through his body. "What! But *why?*"

"She double-crossed Gerard. And they wanted to stop you from helping me."

"Dear God! It was the shock of my life when I found that poor girl in my room—I'm still amazed I escaped the police," Nigel said bitterly. "But there'll be time to clear everything up, Celia. Right now we need to get you to a lifeboat."

"But *Arthur!* Gerard has Arthur!"

We came out on the Boat Deck on the starboard side. The bitter night air was startling—but that surprise was nothing compared to seeing the front of the *Titanic* almost completely under water. The bow lights remained lit underneath the seawater, casting strange reflections and shadows over the gathered crowd. Out in the dark ocean I saw seven or eight lifeboats that looked like little more than faint white dots bobbing in the blackness. Incredibly, there was indeed an orchestra on the deck briskly playing what now sounded like a waltz. The musicians wore strained smiles that made the surrounding confusion that much more frightening.

I was still trying to process how *any* of this was possible when I saw Phil arguing with Emily in front of what seemed to be one of the few remaining lifeboats. The Vogels stood next to them and were having what appeared to be a similar disagreement. Nigel steered me toward them.

"I'm not getting in!" Emily was insisting hysterically. "Not without my father and certainly not until Arthur is found! And—and not without *you!*"

Phil turned to us with a pleading look. "Mr. Bowen! Please talk some sense into her and Mrs. Vogel. So few boats are left!"

Nigel took both Emily and Mrs. Vogel's arms.

"Ladies, you *must* get in," Nigel said forcefully. "And I humbly ask you to tend to my wife."

"Listen to him, my dear," Mr. Vogel begged his wife.

"How can I?" she cried in utter despair. *"I don't know where my son is!"*

I turned to the Vogels, Phil, and Emily. "You're all to get into the lifeboats. Nigel and I will find Arthur. It's *our* responsibility."

I looked at Nigel, and though he began to protest he stopped himself and simply took hold of my hand. He raised it to his mouth and kissed it.

"See here," Phil protested. "I can't agree to that. Why—"

"Nigel and I are *thieves*," I blurted out with exasperation. "I stole your gold watch and he took your bag, Miss Moore. We've cheated at cards and robbed other passengers. And I could have stopped the kidnapping of Arthur but I *didn't*. Nigel and I have much to atone for. So I beg you all—*please* get in the lifeboat!"

Their astonished expressions quickly gave way to further arguing.

Finally, the officer loading the boat brusquely commanded the ladies to either get in the boat or step away from it. Mr. Vogel pressed Phil's hand.

"Please, Mr. Colley," he said. "You're young and perhaps even in love. And the greatest gift you could give me is the peace of mind of knowing my wife is safe and in good hands while I search for our son."

The officer gave the signal to start lowering the boat,

so with a look of pained acceptance, Phil deftly jostled the still-protesting ladies into the craft. Once they were seated, the boat descended and Phil raised his hand in sad farewell. Just before the vessel vanished into the darkness I saw Mrs. Sedgwick staring up at me. There were tears in her eyes.

"Remy!" Nigel shouted.

I turned to see Gerard at the far end of the deck waiting to board a lifeboat—Arthur still in his arms. Mr. Vogel cried with joy at the sight and began running toward them. He dug into his coat pocket and pulled out a slim brick of bills. He waved them at Gerard.

Nigel and I ran after him but two officers who were trying to separate women and children from the men blocked our way. At the sight of Mr. Vogel's money, Gerard pivoted toward him and grabbed the bills. Mr. Vogel used his other hand to reach out for Arthur, but in the entanglement of arms Gerard elbowed Mr. Vogel in his chest. The poor man went reeling backward and fell against the listing rail. He teetered there for a moment, then plunged over into the black ocean.

I screamed in horror.

Gerard gave me a startled glare, then jumped out of the boat line and bolted toward the nearest deck entrance. But just then, a swarm of passengers up from steerage came rushing out. In frustration, Gerard flung little Arthur directly into the mob and began running the other way.

"*Get Arthur!*" I implored Nigel as I ran after Gerard.

I saw him head up past the fourth funnel, clearly heading for a lifeboat on the port side of the ship. He leapt across a rope piling but his foot caught a loop and he fell onto the deck. I threw myself on him.

We struggled and rolled across the floor. All the anger and hurt of the years with him seemed to bubble up inside me and gave me strength I didn't know I had. Taken aback by the ferocity of my attack, he fought me viciously. He straddled my torso and put his hands around my throat. I pounded on his chest and clutched at his clothing. And suddenly I felt the hard metal of his gun in his side coat pocket.

I yanked it out.

As I attempted to take proper hold of the pistol, he tried knocking it out of my hand with his knee. Meanwhile, he increased his brutal choking. I twisted and flailed and felt I was beginning to lose consciousness. But just then I heard a great hissing sound. My eyes flew open, and above his head I saw a distress flare soar gracefully up into the night sky, then explode into a shower of sparks. Startled by the noise and sudden light burst, he involuntarily dropped his guard and looked up.

I shot him squarely in the face.

CHAPTER 29

Nigel Bowen
Atlantic Ocean
Monday, April 15, 1912, 2:05 AM

CELIA HAD DISAPPEARED into the shadows before I could stop her. I turned and shoved my way through the mass of terrified people. It was like battling a tidal wave, especially as we were all fighting the tilt as the ship's front sank lower and the stern began to lift. People were falling and rolling about the deck; I was knocked down and trampled. I had to shove a screaming woman off my pinned leg in order to pull myself to the interior wall.

It was there I saw Davies—and he was clutching Arthur.

The old man was angrily shouting at the people around him—mostly immigrants who probably understood little to no English. *"I have a child here! I must get him to a boat!"* he roared.

I pushed and fought my way through the crowd. Arthur was red-faced and wide-eyed—but not crying. I wondered if he was in some kind of shock.

"Bowen!" Davies cried. "Take the boy. Get him to a boat—they'll let you on if you are with the child!"

"We can *both* take him," I protested, as I scooped Arthur into my arms.

"Don't be a bloody fool!" Davies swore. "I'm an old man. I already got my death sentence today in a telegram. But that doesn't matter. I've lived my life—make sure this boy gets the chance to live *his!*"

His tired eyes beseeched me. "And if you *do* truly love your wife, you won't give up your own life without a fight!"

I put out my hand and he grasped it firmly, then used our clasp to push off from me. Almost immediately, the now thoroughly panicked crowd swallowed him.

Holding Arthur as firmly as possible, I made our way toward the stern. I saw that no boats were left on this side of the ship, so I began making my way over to the other side.

"Where's mommy and daddy?" Arthur asked, sounding both scared and sleepy.

"Your mother is in one of those lifeboats out there," I said as matter-of-factly as I could manage. "So we must get you in one so you can join her when another ship comes by to pick us all up."

I climbed up to the compass platform, which gave me a view of the entire ship; it was now more than halfway under water. And only one lifeboat was left, just past the fourth funnel. I started making my way toward it.

"Nigel!"

Celia staggered out of the shadows. She reached out to

help me hold up the now-sleeping Arthur. There was blood matting her beautiful golden hair.

"You're bleeding!" I cried.

"It's Gerard's. He's dead," she said breathlessly. "It doesn't matter—we must get Arthur to that boat!"

Celia hopped down onto the Boat Deck and took Arthur from my arms. The last small craft was near over-flowing. It contained mostly women, though there were two or three men in it with their children. On deck, a group of men—some terrified, some stoic—were standing by as the officer in charge made one last call for women and children.

"Here!" I cried as I guided Celia and Arthur through the men. Celia halted and pushed Arthur back into my arms.

"*You* take him," she said desperately. "They won't let you on otherwise!"

She started to back away but I grabbed her. "Celia, that's absurd. You must take him to his mother!"

The officer barked out, "Put the child in the boat! We must shove off *now!*"

Celia looked at me wildly and dug her hand into my arm. "Please do this for me, Nigel. I—I love you. I have from nearly the moment we met. But Gerard made me ter-rified of ever caring for anyone again. And so all I've done is lie, cheat, steal, and hurt people. Aside from loving you, my life has been *worthless*—let my death have some value."

"*Never!* Darling, I can't—"

Just then a great crashing noise split the already chaotic night; the funnels were collapsing under pressure from the rising sea. Everyone on deck began screaming and the officer shouted for the lifeboat to be lowered. Celia used the distraction to cut off my protest. Clutching me tightly, she kissed me with unbearably tender passion. Then without looking up, she shoved herself away from me and turned her body around to face the rail.

She dove off the side of the ship.

I bellowed in grief and fury and impulsively started after her, wresting my body toward the rail.

But I still had Arthur in my arms.

Utterly distraught, I started back toward the lifeboat— only to see that it had already lowered.

"Oh, my god," I groaned. I looked around desperately, but I knew already that there were no boats. I had not only lost Celia but I had failed to save Arthur.

The remaining lights on the ship sputtered several times, then went out. I collapsed onto the darkened deck, spent and devoid of hope.

"Where is our boat?" Arthur asked through a yawn. "When do we sail?"

I looked directly into the child's inquisitive eyes. "There are no more boats, Arthur. I'm so sorry, my boy."

Arthur frowned, then looked around.

"Let's build one!" he cried. "We'll put all the deck chairs together and float away on them!"

His excitement broke my heart. He jumped up and began piling collapsed chairs on top of each other. I noticed a tarp that had covered one of the lifeboats lying to the side. The plan was doomed to failure, but I suddenly felt I had to at least try. I quickly gathered up the tarp and flung it over the heap of chairs. I used the ropes that threaded its side to bind the bundle together.

By this point the stern was rising rapidly; we would be pitched into the ocean at any moment. I pulled Arthur on top of the makeshift flotilla and pushed it down the deck to where the water was surging. It hit with a freezing spray, and jumping on top, I used my legs to kick us away from the deck.

The raft initially started to submerge but soon stabilized, and I was able to use a broken chair leg to paddle away from the ship. I rowed and rowed until my arms could take no more. I fell back in exhaustion and finally looked behind us.

I was just in time to see the darkened shell of the *Titanic* take its final plunge under the water.

CHAPTER 30

Nigel Bowen
Atlantic Ocean
Monday, April 15, 1912, 9:10 AM

IN THE DIM morning, I at last saw a hulking gray rescue ship headed our way. I painfully lifted my arm and began waving.

But then I saw that it wasn't a ship after all, just another small but bulky iceberg silently floating by. The ice field was now full of debris from the *Titanic:* clothes, planks, broken furniture, oil slicks, and frozen bodies.

In my desperation to avoid getting sucked under by the ship's plunge, I had rowed us too far beyond the groupings of lifeboats. By the time I realized my mistake, the current had taken us out of their orbit.

Arthur was now curled in my arms, shivering uncontrollably. The tarp we sat on had gotten soaked through and was a sheet of ice. My legs were almost completely numb.

I couldn't keep my head up any longer and looked for a way I might stretch out on our tiny raft. Something in the passing debris caught my eye, and I saw an enormous steamer trunk, half submerged in the water. Another dead body was flung across the top; the frozen hands looked like white claws clutching the sides. I then saw a faint puff of what looked like frosty breath over the person's head. I peered closer. It wasn't breath.

It was the smoke from a large freighter in the distance behind the trunk.

I lurched up, nearly upsetting the rickety raft. I quickly laid Arthur out and grabbed at a white steward shirt that was floating by.

"Ahoy! Over here! Over here!" I yelled as I began furiously waving the wet shirt. I yelled and yelled and finally—miraculously—the ship sounded its horn in acknowledgment. It turned slightly and began heading our way.

My whole body sagged with exhausted relief and I pulled Arthur closer to me. His lips were blue and his skin had a shocking pallor. I leaned in and listened to his shallow breathing; it was clear he wouldn't last much longer. The freighter stopped some distance off and I soon saw the crew lowering a small dinghy to retrieve us. I rubbed Arthur's body as briskly as I could; he just needed to hang on for a little while longer.

I noticed the steamer trunk was now floating off in the other direction. One of the ghostly hands slipped down the side. It was a gruesome sight and I was about to turn away when the arm feebly lifted and sought a corner of the trunk. Incredibly, the person was still alive, if barely. They lifted their head slowly and turned my way.

My shock was equaled only by my joy.

"Celia!"

Her eyelids fluttered weakly; she seemed to be struggling to focus. Finally, her gaze locked with mine and she gave a tiny smile.

I set Arthur down as gently as I could and started frantically paddling the raft in her direction. But the current was far stronger than I had anticipated, or I had finally reached my limit; either way, the raft seemed to hardly move while the steamer trunk drifted past at a gathering speed.

I anxiously looked over to the dinghy—it was directly between us but headed my way. It could conceivably intercept the trunk if I signaled for them to move in the other direction. But wouldn't the delay almost certainly endanger Arthur, who was so desperately in need of immediate medical attention? How could I *possibly* choose?

Again I sagged in defeat. There was no choice. Arthur was a young boy with his whole life ahead of him. And Celia had made her decision.

I watched the trunk drift farther and farther away.

After what seemed like hours, the dinghy finally pulled next to us. Three people sat inside including two crewmen who reached out for Arthur. We made the transfer gingerly so as to not upset the raft. I was relieved to see that the other person in the tiny boat was a doctor. He instantly wrapped the child in a blanket and began tending to him. I turned and searched the area for a sign of Celia and the trunk but there was none.

"You're lucky, mate—probably the last we'll fish out," one of the crew said with his hand outstretched. "Well, come on, then."

I stared at his hand for only a moment. Then—almost without thinking—I turned and began paddling away from them.

"Oy! What's this?" the startled man cried out after me.

I had delivered the boy to safety. I knew there was no chance of saving Celia but I wanted to die trying. That was my choice.

Still using the broken chair leg as an oar, I maneuvered the wobbly craft away from the dinghy and quickly floated into the strong current that had lifted the trunk away. As the bewildered rescuers called after me, I paddled with what little strength I had left.

And, incredibly, within a few moments I saw the trunk again. It had become entangled in an arrested mass of debris that included a section of one of the masts and some kind of rigging. I pushed myself harder and harder, and I soon came upon the wreckage. I carefully poked and prodded my way through the flotsam until I was upon the trunk.

I reached out and took Celia's hand. It was deathly chilled. I tugged her and the trunk closer. I couldn't pull her off—the raft was too small to take on another person, and I didn't dare risk having her fall into the water. I just held her as near as possible and stared into her eyes.

"Your voice," she croaked faintly. "This time I knew *your* cry."

I tried to rub warmth into her hands. She faltered and her eyes fluttered shut. I looked back toward the freighter, but it was now some distance away. Turning slightly, I saw something moving toward us—the dinghy! The crewmen had steered after me! I used my other arm to flag them, and after a moment someone waved back. They would be upon us in minutes.

"Hang on, old girl," I urged Celia. "We made it! We're free!"

She barely opened her eyes and was clearly struggling to stay conscious. I leaned in and gently kissed her. She came around and it seemed to me her face took on a kind of glow.

"But Nigel…our pasts…we're both wanted…"

"No one in America knows our pasts or our names," I assured her. "We'll start over—though without very much, I'm afraid—or, to be more exact, without anything at all. But we'll be together."

Celia began pulling something out of her wool jacket.

Her actions rocked the trunk and I put a hand out to still her. She gave me Emily's small beaded bag and nodded for me to open it. Inside was a folded piece of paper—the check from Davies. Though wrinkled and water stained it had somehow survived her ordeal.

"Throw it in the ocean," Celia said. "That will be our new beginning…"

I looked down at the check that represented so many wrong and painful things in our lives. I was about to quite willingly toss it but then hesitated.

"I'm not sure, Celia…I honestly don't think Davies would have wanted that," I said. "He wanted us to be happy. He wanted us to *live*."

Celia sighed and gave a small rueful laugh. "We'll discuss it later, Mr. Bowen. Our arrangement needs to be renegotiated anyway."

I pulled her into my arms and we floated together silently, listening to the dinghy oars steadily lapping through the water, coming closer and closer and closer. Soon they were directly behind us—as everything was now.

HAVE YOURSELF A SCARY LITTLE CHRISTMAS.

In the heart of the holiday season, priceless paintings have vanished from a Park Avenue murder scene. Now, dashing French detective Luc Moncrief must become a quick study in the art of the steal—before a cold-blooded killer paints the town red.

Merry Christmas, Detective.

Read the thrilling holiday whodunit, coming soon only from

BOOK**SHOTS**

JAMES
PATTERSON
BOOK**SHOTS**
OUT THIS MONTH

KILLER CHEF

Someone is poisoning the diners in New Orleans' best restaurants. Now it's up to chef and homicide cop Caleb Rooney to catch a killer set on revenge.

DAZZLING: **THE DIAMOND TRILOGY, PART 1**

To support her artistic career, Siobhan Dempsey works at the elite Stone Room in New York City... never expecting to be swept away by tech billionaire Derick Miller.

BODYGUARD

Special Agent Abbie Whitmore has only one task: protect Congressman Jonathan Lassiter from a violent cartel's threats. Yet she's never had to do it while falling in love...

JAMES PATTERSON

BOOK**SHOTS**

COMING SOON

THE CHRISTMAS MYSTERY

Two priceless paintings disappear from a Park Avenue murder scene –
French detective Luc Moncrief is in for a not-so-merry Christmas.

COME AND GET US

Miranda Cooper's life takes a terrifying turn when an SUV deliberately
runs her and her husband off a desolate Arizona road.

RADIANT: THE DIAMOND TRILOGY, PART 2

Siobhan has moved to Detroit following her traumatic break-up
with Derick, but when Derick comes after her, Siobhan must decide
whether she can trust him again...

HOT WINTER NIGHTS

Allie Fairchild made a mistake when she moved to Montana, but just
when she's about to throw in the towel, life in Bear Mountain takes a
surprisingly sexy turn...

BOOKSHOTS

STORIES AT THE SPEED OF LIFE

www.bookshots.com

ALSO BY JAMES PATTERSON

ALEX CROSS NOVELS
Along Came a Spider
Kiss the Girls
Jack and Jill
Cat and Mouse
Pop Goes the Weasel
Roses are Red
Violets are Blue
Four Blind Mice
The Big Bad Wolf
London Bridges
Mary, Mary
Cross
Double Cross
Cross Country
Alex Cross's Trial (*with Richard DiLallo*)
I, Alex Cross
Cross Fire
Kill Alex Cross
Merry Christmas, Alex Cross
Alex Cross, Run
Cross My Heart
Hope to Die
Cross Justice
Cross the Line

THE WOMEN'S MURDER CLUB SERIES
1st to Die
2nd Chance (*with Andrew Gross*)
3rd Degree (*with Andrew Gross*)
4th of July (*with Maxine Paetro*)
The 5th Horseman (*with Maxine Paetro*)
The 6th Target (*with Maxine Paetro*)

7th Heaven (*with Maxine Paetro*)
8th Confession (*with Maxine Paetro*)
9th Judgement (*with Maxine Paetro*)
10th Anniversary (*with Maxine Paetro*)
11th Hour (*with Maxine Paetro*)
12th of Never (*with Maxine Paetro*)
Unlucky 13 (*with Maxine Paetro*)
14th Deadly Sin (*with Maxine Paetro*)
15th Affair (*with Maxine Paetro*)

DETECTIVE MICHAEL BENNETT SERIES
Step on a Crack (*with Michael Ledwidge*)
Run for Your Life (*with Michael Ledwidge*)
Worst Case (*with Michael Ledwidge*)
Tick Tock (*with Michael Ledwidge*)
I, Michael Bennett (*with Michael Ledwidge*)
Gone (*with Michael Ledwidge*)
Burn (*with Michael Ledwidge*)
Alert (*with Michael Ledwidge*)
Bullseye (*with Michael Ledwidge*)

PRIVATE NOVELS
Private (*with Maxine Paetro*)
Private London (*with Mark Pearson*)
Private Games (*with Mark Sullivan*)
Private: No. 1 Suspect (*with Maxine Paetro*)
Private Berlin (*with Mark Sullivan*)
Private Down Under (*with Michael White*)
Private L.A. (*with Mark Sullivan*)

Private India (*with Ashwin Sanghi*)
Private Vegas (*with Maxine Paetro*)
Private Sydney (*with Kathryn Fox*)
Private Paris (*with Mark Sullivan*)
The Games (*with Mark Sullivan*)

NYPD RED SERIES
NYPD Red (*with Marshall Karp*)
NYPD Red 2 (*with Marshall Karp*)
NYPD Red 3 (*with Marshall Karp*)
NYPD Red 4 (*with Marshall Karp*)

STAND-ALONE THRILLERS
Sail (*with Howard Roughan*)
Swimsuit (*with Maxine Paetro*)
Don't Blink (*with Howard Roughan*)
Postcard Killers (*with Liza Marklund*)
Toys (*with Neil McMahon*)
Now You See Her (*with Michael Ledwidge*)
Kill Me If You Can (*with Marshall Karp*)
Guilty Wives (*with David Ellis*)
Zoo (*with Michael Ledwidge*)
Second Honeymoon (*with Howard Roughan*)
Mistress (*with David Ellis*)
Invisible (*with David Ellis*)
The Thomas Berryman Number
Truth or Die (*with Howard Roughan*)

Murder House (*with David Ellis*)
Never Never (*with Candice Fox*)
Woman of God (*with Maxine Paetro*)

BOOKSHOTS
Black & Blue (*with Candice Fox*)
Break Point (*with Lee Stone*)
Cross Kill
Private Royals (*with Rees Jones*)
The Hostage (*with Robert Gold*)
Zoo 2 (*with Max DiLallo*)
Heist (*with Rees Jones*)
Hunted (*with Andrew Holmes*)
Airport: Code Red (*with Michael White*)
The Trial (*with Maxine Paetro*)
Little Black Dress (*with Emily Raymond*)
Chase (*with Michael Ledwidge*)
Let's Play Make-Believe (*with James O. Born*)
Dead Heat (*with Lee Stone*)
Triple Threat
113 Minutes (*with Max DiLallo*)
The Verdict (*with Robert Gold*)
French Kiss (*with Richard DiLallo*)
$10,000,000 Marriage Proposal (*with Hilary Liftin*)
Kill or Be Killed